Clayton Hanson

Five
Seventy - Four
Press

ALSO BY CLAYTON HANSON

AFTER SUNSET

Ms. Remorse

A Novel

Clayton Hanson

For my mother. One book isn't enough and neither is two.

ACKNOWLEDGMENTS

I would like to thank:
Emily Ethridge for her encouragement, support, and amazing
edits. Obviously.
My brother Coby Hanson, my father Gary Hanson, Sara
Bondioli, Chris Foster, Pat Joy, Kaitie Kovach and Anna Miller.

I long for home, long for the sight of home. If any god has marked me out again for shipwreck, my tough heart can undergo it.
What hardship have I not long since endured at sea, in battle. Let the trial come. – Homer, The Odyssey

Clayton Hanson

6 WEEKS BEFORE THE CAPTAIN'S LAST SEASON

Nick walked into the bank wearing slacks, a button-up and a baseball cap. Before he had left the house he had checked to make sure that the tattoo on his right forearm wasn't visible. The police had photographed it plenty of times. It wouldn't take them long to find him in the FBI database. His beard was longer than it had ever been before, and he couldn't wait to shave it off. Letting his dark brown hair and beard grow was the easiest way to blend in as a local in Santa Fe and his facial hair helped hide his chiseled chin. During his four and a half months there, Nick had learned the city was one of the last stopping points before children of the 60s went to the big Woodstock in the sky. All he needed was to wear Teva sandals, tan shorts and a Hawaiian print shirt and his assimilation was complete.

Weeks of planning were at stake. There are very few moments (if any) in a person's life when he puts everything on the line. This was his.

The bank was a typical regional chain, with posters advertising mortgage rates and a few pieces of locally inspired mass-produced art on the wall. The manager's glassed-in office was in the back to the right. Next to it was a vault with a metal fence across the entrance. The teller stations served as a kind of barricade between the customers and the office/vault area.

The manager stood next to a teller who Nick knew to be Anna. She pointed at something on Anna's computer. Nick shuffled his way through the velvet rope maze used to corral customers. He stood next to the "Please Wait Here" sign until Anna smiled and waved him over. The manager smiled at him, then retreated to her office.

Nick had waited until the other teller, Sandra, went to lunch. Sandra didn't have children so he didn't have any use for her. After watching the bank for three weeks he knew that Sandra averaged a thirty-seven minute lunch break. He had twenty-nine minutes left.

As Nick approached Anna, he almost chickened out. He felt bad about what he was going to do to such a smiley woman. He didn't want to snuff out the light that was the internal source of her beauty. Anna was pretty like the neighborhood girl he had a crush on growing up. Anna's face was a deep tan unachievable from a tanning bed, and her dark brown hair was dyed blond by the sun in several places.

Loud enough for the manager to hear he said, "Don't I know you? Your daughter Isabella is in the same class at Wood-Gormley Elementary as my son, James."

"Which class is he in?" asked Anna. She knew that she hadn't met him before, but her years in customer service had trained her to smile and be polite.

The manager got up and shut the door to her office. She gave another obligatory smile, though it appeared to Nick that she was baring her teeth at him. Nick thought that he couldn't have planned that any better.

"I would like to cash this," Nick said, sliding a piece of paper across the desk. He kept his hands in plain sight of the cameras so she couldn't say it was armed robbery. Using a firearm would add a mandatory five years to his sentence if he got caught.

Anna looked at the piece of paper, then at Nick. Tears welled in her light gray eyes. Nick put his messenger bag on top of the teller station, but kept it hidden from the manager's sight.

"Please don't hurt her," Anna whispered. The note said that Isabella was at recess and that Nick's partner had his rifle scoped on her. If Anna didn't obey Nick's orders, her daughter would die. The note also said that the money was insured by the FDIC and that she wouldn't be held responsible for it, so she shouldn't try to be a hero.

"We don't want to hurt your daughter, Anna." She winced when he said her name. "We just want the money. Your daughter's life is in your hands." Nick put his phone on the desk for emphasis. "One call."

Nick watched Anna transform from having a good day to the worst day of her life in moments. "We need you to give us ten minutes after we leave, okay? If you don't, then bad things are going to happen."

Anna pulled the money out and placed the stacks between them.

"Is there an ink bomb in one of these?" Nick said, forcing himself to look pleasant in case the manager was watching. Anna didn't indicate either way. Her breathing was shallow.

"I hope not. For your sake." He paused and looked into Anna's eyes, trying to get a read on her. She was a blank slate. "And Isabella's."

Anna reached across the desk and pulled one of the stacks of bills back to her.

When he had all of the money from her drawer, he strapped his messenger bag around his shoulder and walked out. His instinct was to run as fast as he could but he didn't want to attract attention.

Once outside, he walked to his bike parked around the corner and rode through the twisting and turning paths that led to the plaza in the center of town.

From the plaza he headed a few blocks south to the Inn at Loretto. The tan building was built with traditional New Mexican flair, built in different blocks of varying heights, with wooden support beams sticking out of the top of each block. The first time he saw the building, and most of the architecture in New Mexico for that matter, he thought the overuse of tan and turquoise was tacky, but now it had grown on him.

He entered through the side, knowing that if he came through the main entrance, no fewer than three members of the hotel staff would have greeted him. He walked down a long, beige hallway lined with silver artifacts in glass cases to the restrooms. Inside, he locked the door. He took off his dress shirt, hat and slacks. Underneath his slacks he was wearing khaki shorts. Standing there shirtless, he turned on a set of cordless beard trimmers and shaved his chestnut-colored beard off in less than thirty seconds. He moved as fast as he could. When he was done he looked like he hadn't shaved in a few days instead of a few months. He ran some water through his hair to get rid of his hat head, then splashed some water around the sink to clean it out. Even though he wasn't a neat freak, he knew the less evidence of him being there the better. He pulled on a tee shirt from the Institute of American Indian Arts and changed from dress shoes into flip-flops. His conversion from local to another tourist in a sea of vacationers was complete. He stuffed his robbery clothes, as he thought of them, into his messenger bag and put the messenger bag and the money into his backpack.

Once outside he went around to the back, pulled out the messenger bag, looked to see if anyone was watching, and tossed it into a dumpster. His bicycle was the last piece of his robbery gear. He took it to a half-full bike rack, wiped it down for fingerprints, and left it there unlocked.

For the first time in a long time, he smiled. Not the simple smile that he used in social situations. It was a smile that came from inside. It was the same smile he had after picking up a lady at a bar, or when he made a great play in one of the many sports he played in high school. It was the grin of success. He wasn't even aware of his smile because his adrenaline was pumping so hard that he could feel his heartbeat behind his eyes. The rush was more intoxicating than any drug he had tried.

He strolled down the sidewalk in the shining sun. In Santa Fe, the sun felt closer than it did at his home in Alaska. He felt like he had just claimed his piece of the world.

He went into one of the many restaurants overlooking the plaza. The lunch crowd was dissipating and he was able to get a table outside on the patio. He wanted an excuse to keep his sunglasses on, and he might be able to get a head start if the police showed up looking for him.

Nick looked down at the obelisk in the center of the square. Tourists posed for pictures outside the knee-high fence that surrounded it. The monument had been dedicated in 1868 to "The heroes who have fallen in the various battles with the savage Indians in the Territory of New Mexico." Nick had learned from reading about the area that in the '70s, someone had chiseled out the word "savages" from the dedication. He didn't know if it was a native from the area or just a random person but he appreciated civil disobedience nevertheless.

He ordered a margarita on the rocks without salt and queso dip. The short, red-haired waitress gave him goo-goo eyes and he considered pursuing her but didn't want to push his luck. He had $9,000 in his backpack, and that made him happier than a fling with the waitress ever would. Also, he realized, it was a bad idea to make a new friend when he was leaving soon.

There had been a time when all he had cared about was picking up women. But contrary to what many guys believe (mainly married guys), that lifestyle eventually lead to boredom. There were nights when he longed for a steady woman who knew him, so he wouldn't have get to know someone new every time he wanted to hook up. He still enjoyed the pursuit, but the thrill wasn't what it used to be.

He had two margaritas, enough to get a buzz going, ate some of the dip and walked the mile to his grandmother's house. It was hard for him to shake the feeling that everyone was looking at him, even if logically he knew that they weren't.

If someone were to ask him why he robbed the bank, he would say that he did it to see if he could get away with it, or because of the thrill, but neither of these reasons was true. He had a debt to repay.

26 YEARS BEFORE THE CAPTAIN'S LAST SEASON

On his way to school, Nick bent down to grab a snowball to throw at a stop sign when he saw a scar on the back of his hand. It reminded him of the first time his Uncle Robert hit him. It was a simple slap upside his head. His uncle hadn't made a fist or else Nick would've been knocked out.

Instead, the blow had brought Nick to one knee, causing him to drag the back of his hand on the corner of the stove door. He had tried to regain his sight, expecting a follow-up attack, but Robert had left the kitchen of their trailer and walked into the living room like nothing had happened.

He pulled up his coat to get his collar to protect his ears from the fall wind that came whipping through the Eagle River valley. The more he struggled not to think about it, the stronger the memory came back.

After the blow Nick had sat in the corner of the kitchen and cried quietly while covering his hand with a dish towel. He knew that any noise might set off his uncle, who had already threatened to give him something to cry about.

Even in his seven-year old mind, he knew that if he had had a gun he wouldn't have had a problem killing his uncle. He hadn't done anything to provoke the attack. He had been hurt by someone who was supposed to protect him.

He had lived with his aunt and uncle since he was three, and he knew they didn't like him. When he was five, his aunt told him that if they had wanted "a damn rug monkey" they would've had one of their own.

A dog barking in the distance brought him back to the present. He kicked a rock. It skipped once and hit the side of a car down the street with a loud tick. He looked around to make sure no one was watching.

He had always wanted a dog of his own, but that was the kind of thing that fathers gave to sons. His dad had stuck around for the first few years after he was born. Nick sometimes thought that he had vague memories of him, but he wasn't sure. His aunt Amy said that he went out for a pack of smokes and never came back. Nick thought that maybe he was making up the memories in his head because he wanted to have them so badly.

After his mom killed herself, his memories became even more scrambled. He combined the meager memories of his father with the few actual memories of his mother in an effort to create a feeling of family but it never worked.

Nick put on a smile and shoved all of it out of his mind when he opened the door to school.

25 YEARS BEFORE THE CAPTAIN'S LAST SEASON

The cop saw the boy walking down the street alone. At first he didn't think much of it, but when Officer Williams got closer he could see the boy's little shoulders shaking and his hands covering his face. He rolled up next to the boy and saw a lump on the side of the boy's head.

Williams pulled ahead and got out of the car. He had the build of a high school running back who had put on a few extra pounds since graduating. The boy turned around and started to walk in the other direction.

"Hey little man," Williams said. "Why don't you come over here and talk to me for a minute?"

Williams phrased it as a question, but it was clearly an order. That was the way he had been taught at the academy. As a recent graduate who had finished the partner ride portion of his training the week before, he still had all the lessons fresh in his head.

The lanky brown-haired boy took a few steps toward him, still covering his face.

"What's your name?" Williams tried to sound as nice as he could. He knew that a man with a gun was intimidating enough.

"Nick," the boy said.

"Can you move your hands please? It's hard to hear you through them."

Nick slowly put his hands down while watching Williams's eyes. Williams tried not to flinch when he saw not only the bulge on the boy's head, but also a welt under one eye and dried blood that had dribbled to his mouth from his nostrils. A lump formed in Williams's throat, and with a deep breath he composed himself. He knew that this was more than some neighborhood fight between kids.

"Who did this to you?" Williams asked in almost a whisper.

"No one," Nick replied, looking everywhere but at Williams.

"You can either tell me here or we can go down to the station and call your parents."

When Williams said the word 'parents', the boy started to cry again. Tears fell on his tattered blue Superman shirt.

"I don't have parents. They're gone."

"Gone where?"

"Dead, gone. I live with my Uncle Robert and Aunt Amy."

"Did they do this to you?"

"My Uncle Robert did."

"Does he do this a lot?"

"Yeah. I dunno. Sometimes."

"Okay," Williams pulled a pen out of his pocket. "Can you follow this pen with your eyes please?"

Williams watched his eyes. Up, down, right, left. It was a test to see if someone was drunk but Williams was trying to buy himself a little time. He wanted the boy to think about something other than his dead parents. He knew that turning the child over to protective services could be even worse for the boy.

"Do you feel sick?"

Williams knew if the boy had nausea or any other concussion indicators he had learned about, he would have to take him to the hospital.

"No."

"Any ringing in your ears?"

"No. He didn't hit me in my ears."

"Okay, last thing. Can you stand on one leg?" The boy's balance seemed fine but he wanted to make sure. "Now howl like a dog."

"What?" Nick said cautiously. He put his foot down. He was used to dealing with people who had a few loose screws, and the cop made him nervous.

"You know, like this, owwwwww."

Nick looked at Williams for a moment, cleared his throat, and let out a soulful "Owwwwwww."

It was the loneliest sound that Williams had ever heard.

"Okay, okay. It sounds like you're fine."

The boy finally smiled.

"Do you want to go for a ride?" Williams didn't know what to do. His shift commander was an old hard-ass who would tell him to hand the boy over to the state.

"In the front or the back?" Nick asked.

Williams was surprised at the question. He wondered if the boy had been in the back before.

"In the front."

"Cool."

Williams went around to the driver's side and got in. He reached across and opened the passenger door. The boy looked smaller when he was riding shotgun. Nick's eyes stared at all of the gadgets, trying to take it all in.

"Don't say anything for a minute," Williams said to Nick, and then picked up his CB. "Williams to station."

"Go ahead Williams," replied a female voice.

"I'm going to grab lunch. Just a heads up."

"No problem, Williams. We'll have Ethridge cover the calls. Are you going to Garcias for the millionth time? You must have guts of steel to eat Mexican food every day." The lady giggled.

"Negative. I'm going to McDonald's."

Nick's eyes lit up. Williams returned his look with a grin.

"That's even worse, Williams. Enjoy yourself."

"Thanks." Williams leaned over and put the CB back into its holder.

"All right Nick. Do you want to go to McDonald's with me? My treat."

"Sure."

Williams was trying to soften the blow of telling the boy that he was going to take him home because it was the best of all of the bad options. Williams knew what it was like to have a parental figure who got rough with kids, but in his case it had been his mother.

"Hey pal. Why don't you flip that switch to turn on the lights, and that one to turn on the siren?"

"Really?" Nick was grinning ear to ear.

"Sure. Why not?"

The moment Williams had finished his "sure," Nick flipped the switches and the car immediately felt authoritative, a vehicle equipped for war.

"Hold on," Williams said as he stepped on the gas.

They flew down the block. They were only going 45 mph but with the tight turns of the neighborhood, it felt like 100. The force of the car caused them to lean into the corners. When they got to the main thoroughfare, Williams turned the switches off.

"Don't tell anyone we did that, okay?"

"Uh huh." Nick's eyes were lit up. Williams knew that this kid was going to tell everyone he met for the next year or two what had happened, but he didn't mind.

They pulled into the McDonald's drive-thru lane.

"All right little man," Williams said. "Do you know what you want?"

"Two cheeseburgers, ketchup only, a small fry and a Coke."

Williams smiled. "All right then."

He pulled up, paid the cashier, and they drove out of the parking lot. Williams turned into a strip mall lot and parked his car facing the street.

"People are going to think we're checking their speed so once they see us, they'll slow down," he explained. "Watch."

They watched the cars go by. Some cruised at the same speed even after seeing the cop car, but a majority slammed on their brakes, their taillights betraying their indiscretion. A green Honda flew down the street, and the driver slammed the brakes with so much force that the car leaned forward.

"Whoa," Nick said, with his mouth full of fries. "Did you see that?"

"Should we flash the lights at him?"

"Yeah."

"Hit 'em."

Nick hit the light switch. The flashers came on and the Honda slowed down even more. Then Williams turned the lights off.

"I think he'll drive slower for the rest of the day," he said.

Nick nodded in agreement, his mouth stuffed with cheeseburger.

Williams grabbed his quarter pounder out of the bag and pulled his Coke from the travel tray. By the time he had unwrapped his burger, Nick had finished his first and was well on his way with the second.

It was hard for Williams to eat, knowing that he had to bring the boy home. Williams had firsthand experience with the foster system and knew it might put the boy in a worse situation than if the state kept him at his house.

Williams took a small bite of his burger. Nick had finished both of his and was searching the bag for wayward fries.

"So pal," Williams said. "I'm going to have to take you home after we eat, okay?"

"Yeah," Nick responded without looking up from the bag.

"I'm going to talk to your uncle and maybe that will help."

"Okay. Maybe it will." Nick said without a trace of hope in his voice.

Williams put half of his burger back in the bag. He couldn't stomach any more, and it wasn't due to the quality of the beef. He had to prepare himself to talk to some asshole who thought it was okay to wail on kids. All of a sudden being a cop didn't seem like such a great career choice.

"Are you done with that?" Nick said, looking sheepish and a little brave at the same time. He didn't make eye contact with Williams when he asked. His eyes were focused on the bag.

"Want it?" Williams wondered if the boy wasn't being fed at home or if that was typical boy behavior.

Nick didn't say a word. He fished the half-eaten burger out of the bag, unwrapped it and started in on it.

"Where do you live?" Williams asked.

"Banff Park, number 9," Nick said through the burger.

Banff Park was the only trailer park in town. Locals called it Barf Park. Half of them were referring to the amount of alcoholics that lived there and the other half were referring to the fact that it was an eyesore in an otherwise upper-middle class town.

They pulled out of the parking lot and drove over to the park.

After almost running over a mangy dog, they pulled into the driveway of the #9 trailer. A man in a green University of Alaska Anchorage tee shirt came outside on the porch. His forearms were sinewy as if they were made of a pale whip and his teeth were brown and sparse. He eyed Nick and Officer Williams as they got out of the car.

"What did he do now?" the man asked.

"He didn't do anything," Williams said. "Nick, why don't you go inside?"

"Don't give him orders, you son of a bitch," the man barked.

"Easy with the language, friend," Williams said and nodded at Nick to go into the house.

Nick went up the stairs with his head ducked low, expecting a blow. The man flinched at Nick and the boy ducked and ran inside.

"Your name is Robert, right?" Williams said.

"What's it to you?" Robert came down off the porch. He walked toward Williams until there was less than five feet between them.

"I'm just making sure that I know I'm talking to the right guy," Williams said, putting his hand on his baton. "I'm not looking for trouble, but what you did to that boy isn't necessary and you know it."

"How in the hell do you know what's necessary?" Robert moved a little closer, clenching and unclenching his fists.

"You don't got to beat a boy to get him to listen." Williams took a slow half-step toward Robert. Later he would regret elevating the situation by countering aggression with aggression, but he didn't regret what he did next.

"I might have to beat you to get you to listen," Robert snarled.

Williams pulled out his baton and swung it down, connecting a few inches above Robert's right knee. If he had hit the knee, the bone would have shattered, but instead he caught the meat of the leg.

Robert fell on his side, holding his right leg and moaning.

"Don't threaten an officer," Williams said. "And leave that boy alone."

"Fuck you," Robert said through gritted teeth.

"If I have to come back, you'll wish I didn't."

Robert lay there groaning, glaring at Williams.

Williams got in his car and drove off. He wondered if he would last as an officer.

24 YEARS BEFORE THE CAPTAIN'S LAST SEASON

A slight breeze sent a chill through Tom's jacket while he was taking his yellow lab, Trixie, for a walk. It was early spring and the pussy willows were beginning to sprout their buds. Tom had returned earlier in the week from the opilio crab season that starts in late January. The season lasted about six weeks counting the time it took to drop the crab off at the processors and docking the boat in Seattle. As he strolled through the woods, he heard a bunch of boys teasing someone down the street. Although he couldn't make out the words, their voices had an incendiary tone. When Tom emerged from the woods he recognized his nine-year-old son's backpack and shaggy blond hair. Tom was about to yell but held his tongue. He wanted to run over there and whip the tar out of the bullies, but he knew that they would just catch his boy when he wasn't there to save him. And next time it might be worse. If it got out of hand now, one good shout would send the attackers running. Bullies were only tough when they had the clear advantage.

Out of the corner of his eye he saw movement. A brown-haired boy about Max's size had put down all but one of his books and was jogging toward the other boys, using the cars parked on the side of the road to conceal his approach.

One boy pushed Max to the ground and the others swarmed around him. The brown-haired ragamuffin went into a full sprint and clobbered one of the bullies in the back of his head with the book. From fifty yards away, Tom thought that he heard the thump. The bully fell forward to his knees and started crying. Another bully turned to run, but the boy dropped his book and jumped on his back like a lion attacking an elephant.

In the meantime, Max had got off the ground, taken off his backpack, and kicked the book-thumped boy in the ribs. Tom knew he would have to talk to his son about putting the boots to a man while he was down, but he figured a little bit in this case was okay.

Then Max ran and plowed into the brown-haired boy and the bully who was still standing. All three of them fell. After a momentary scrum, the larger boy got free and the three boys got up at the same time. The bully backed away slowly. It was a tentative truce.

Max and his defender looked around for more attackers. Seeing none, they collected their belongings. Tom hustled home and started to make a sandwich in the kitchen.

When Max came in, he brought the other boy with him. He was even dirtier up close, thanks in part to the tussling on the ground. Max had the makings of a little black eye.

The little warriors had small scrapes and scratches but nothing life-threatening. Carol wasn't going to be happy, but Tom would do his best to talk her down. Even though it had scared the shit out of him to watch his son get into a fight, he was proud of Max. He hoped that it would be the last fight Max would get in.

"Dad, this is Nick," Max said, with a slight adrenaline-fueled tremble in his voice.

"Hi buddy," Tom said to his son, ruffling his hair. "Hey Nick. What do you say? You boys hungry?"

Max shrugged his shoulders and looked at Nick, who nodded yes. "Sure," Max said.

"Good deal," Tom said. He wanted to talk about the fight but didn't want to push. He rubbed the chin hair of his beard out of habit. "Hey little man, what happened to your eye?"

"I dunno," Max said with a grin at Nick.

"Are you sure you don't know?" Tom loved that his son was a horrible liar.

"Um, yes." The boys started to giggle.

"All right then," Tom replied. He turned back to the counter and began to make them sandwiches.

23 YEARS BEFORE THE CAPTAIN'S LAST SEASON

Max was dreaming about being stranded alone on a rock when he heard a sharp pop on the side of his house. He was in the hinterland between sleep and being awake when he heard it again, this time much louder and off his window. He froze. From outside he heard a soft voice.

"Max," the voice said. "Maxie Pad."

He sat up confused. There was only one person who called him that. He got out of bed and looked out his second-story window. Nick stood in the backyard with a hood pulled over his head and a baseball cap. Max slowly opened the window and looked back at his door to make sure that his parents weren't coming in.

"Hey," Nick said in a breathless whisper-shout. "Can I stay here tonight?"

"What?" Max said. He was still confused about why he was talking to his best friend out his window at 2 a.m..

"Can I stay the night? I can leave before anyone gets up."

"Meet me at the back door."

"Okay," Nick whispered.

A few moments later, Max opened the back door and Trixie the yellow lab ran out in the yard to greet Nick. Max motioned for Nick to come inside. Max was glad that his dog knew Nick so she didn't bark and wake his parents.

"What's going on?" Max asked. He liked his friend but getting out of bed in the middle of the night while his parents slept made him anxious about getting in trouble.

"My uncle..." Nick said.

"Okay," Max said, thinking for a moment. "Let's go upstairs. Be quiet okay?"

Nick nodded then shivered. It was a long, cold walk between his house and Max's house in the winter.

They crept around the house like cartoon burglars, overemphasizing each movement and freezing when the floor creaked.

When they got to the bedroom, Max shut the door. He put a rolled-up towel against the crack at the bottom of the door and took a flashlight from his desk drawer. He turned it on, cupping his hand over it to dim the light.

He jumped when he saw Nick's face in the light. His right eye was raw and red surrounded by a growing blue welt on the underside. A cut above his left eye was bleeding.

"Are you okay?" Max said. All of a sudden he didn't know if Nick should be over. He wondered if his parents were going to be mad or if Nick's crazy uncle was going to come after him.

"I have a headache but I'll be all right."

Max was stunned about how calm his friend was.

"Stay here," he ordered Nick. "Don't move. I'll be right back."

Nick didn't say anything. He sat on the floor, amazed at all the neat stuff that Max had. No matter how many times he came over, he was still jealous of Max's cool things. Nick couldn't believe that Max had a Nintendo with more than thirty games and a TV in his room. If Nick lived here, he wouldn't ever leave.

Max came back in the room with a bag of peas, some bandages and a bottle of rubbing alcohol.

"Lay down on the bed," Max said, "and put this on your eye."

"What?" Nick was confused. "Peas? I don't like peas."

"No one likes peas," Max replied. He didn't want any backtalk from his patient. "It'll help your eye. Mom always puts it on my bruises."

Nick leaned back and put the bag on his eye. He winced and then slowly laid the bag down, testing its pressure and getting used to how cold it was.

"This is going to hurt a little bit."

"What is?" Nick was scared for the first time since arriving.

Nick started to sit up but Max softly pushed him back down on the bed.

"This alcohol stuff. Mom always puts it on my cuts before putting on a bandage. It's so that you won't get an infection. If you get one, they'll cut off whatever is infected."

"They would cut off my head if I got an infection?"

"I don't know. Maybe just your forehead. Then again, with your face it might be an improvement."

Nick laughed a little, cautiously because it hurt his face.

Max continued, "I'm not sure how it works but either way it doesn't seem like a good idea."

Max poured a little alcohol on a cotton ball and then set the bottle down on his nightstand.

"On three, ready?"

"Yep."

"One."

Max pressed the ball of cotton on Nick's cut.

"Ow, ow, ow, ow, ow."

Nick flexed his back, trying to get away, but Max had anticipated his move and held him still until he stopped squirming. Then he pulled it off.

"You said three, dicknose."

"I know," Max said. "One was just easier."

"Dicknose."

Max put the bandage over the cut.

"See? Your cut is all better now."

"It doesn't feel better."

"At least they won't amputate your head now."

"They should amputate your head," Nick said.

"Don't be a baby." Max smiled at Nick. "Stay there while the peas do their magic. I'll take the pillow and lay on the floor for a while."

Max made himself comfortable on the floor. He wanted to stay up and ask Nick about what had happened, but once his head hit the pillow he fell asleep.

Tom woke up before Carol and had a cup of coffee. His crab fisherman father had trained him to wake up at the crack of dawn since he was a teenager. Now that he ran the crab boat it wasn't in his nature to sleep in.

After a few cups, he went upstairs to ask his son if he wanted to go out fishing on Mirror Lake. He opened the bedroom door slowly and saw his son sprawled on the floor. He started to walk in to pick him up when he saw Nick sleeping in his son's bed.

He thought Nick looked like he had spent the night in a punching bag. Tom looked around the room and saw the first aid kit, rubbing alcohol, and peas surrounded by a wet ring on the carpet.

He wanted to wake them both up and find out what had happened, but decided that Nick had probably been embarrassed enough for one night. He closed the door and stepped away.

Tom went back downstairs and read the paper, thinking about what he was supposed to do.

A short time later Max came downstairs, saw his dad in the kitchen and went back upstairs.

Then Max walked back down the stairs and over to his dad.

"Hey Dad," Max said. "Can I show you something?"

"Sure," Tom said. "What is it, son?"

"It's in the garage."

"Oh," Tom responded. He was hoping that his son was going to tell him what had happened, but he wasn't going to pry it out of him while Nick was still upstairs. "Sure."

He got up and followed his son out to the garage.

"What's up?" Tom asked. He heard the back door open and then shut softly.

"I...forgot," Max said, looking away from his dad.
"Okay. If you remember, let me know, all right?"
"I will."
"No matter what it is."
"Okay, Dad."

22 YEARS BEFORE THE CAPTAIN'S LAST SEASON

Nick and Max went into the Quick Stop on their way home from school. They were discussing their favorite treats in the candy aisle when Max looked around, reached down, and put a square-shaped PB-Max candy bar into his bag. Nick was surprised, but he tried to play it cool. As they were walking out, a burly, bearded store clerk moved in front of the glass doors. Nick fought the urge to cry.

"Give me the bag," the man said. He pulled the backpack out of Max's hand. Nick dropped his books and pulled on the backpack. It was a short game of tug of war that Nick lost.

"It's mine," Nick said.

"This is your book bag?" asked the clerk, holding it up.

"Yes," Nick said. "Can I have it back?"

"No." The clerk shook his head. "Why was he carrying it?"

"I tricked him into carrying it."

"Is this true?" the clerk said to Max.

Max nodded yes. He wanted to tell the truth but found himself unable.

"All right." The man put his hand on Max's back and led him out the door.

"You leave. You," he called back to Nick, "sit."

Max walked down the street and sat on a tree stump where he could see the store. He wanted to go back and tell the man that he did it, and to let Nick go, but he didn't want to get in trouble. He didn't want to disappoint his father. A short time later a police cruiser pulled up in front of the Quick Stop. The cop went in and came out with Nick, who was carrying his books and wearing Max's backpack.

Nick got in the back of the cruiser and the officer got in the front. They pulled out of the store and drove past Max. Max gave Nick a small wave. Nick returned the greeting by smiling, but with a terrified look in his eyes.

Max walked on a trail through the woods on the way home. Fluorescent orange surveyor sticks dotted the woods along the path, marking where a new neighborhood was going to be built adjacent to his parents'. He pulled one of them out of the ground.

Purple fireweeds grew three feet tall next to the trail and Max started using the stick as a sword to chop them down. He swung as hard as he could at a solitary flower. For a moment the flower hung suspended, as if it didn't know that it had been cut, then it floated to the ground.

Max looked down at the flower and started to cry. He knew that if Nick were there they would have made a game out of chopping down the flowers, but instead he was alone and feeling guilty.

Nick felt like a villain from one of Max's comic books in the back of the cruiser. It wasn't nearly as fun as riding in front with Officer Williams.

"Nick, what's your last name?" asked the officer.

"Ferris," Nick responded.

The officer picked up the CB. "Station this is Hornburg."

"Go ahead Hornburg," a woman replied.

"I got the shoplifter from Quick Stop. White, male, eleven years old. His name is Nick Ferris. I'm going to take him home and see what his parents say. There's no reason to escalate at this point."

"Roger that. Let us know when you are finished."

Hornburg had just put the CB back into its holder on the dashboard when it chirped again.

"Williams to Hornburg."

When Nick heard Williams's voice, he sat up.

"Yeah, buddy," Hornburg said.

"I know that kid," Williams said. "Can I talk to him before you take him home?"

"Aren't you off today?"

"Yep. Meet me at the Ravenswood sign."

"All right. See you in ten." Hornburg hung up the CB.

When Hornburg and Nick arrived, Williams was standing outside of his car in plainclothes waiting for them. Hornburg got out of the car and talked to Williams for a moment, then came back and let Nick out. The two of them walked over to Williams, who was standing next to his car, glaring.

"Hi," Nick said feebly.

Williams continued to scowl at him. "Tell Officer Hornburg who your uncle is."

Nick looked at Hornburg. "Robert Thompson."

After a second of thought, Hornburg said, "Holy shit. Your uncle is Robert Thompson?"

"Hey, watch the language," Williams barked.

"I'm sure this kid has heard "shit" before," Hornburg said. "What's your uncle going to do when he finds out that you got caught shoplifting?"

"I dunno," Nick said. "I've never been caught."

Hornburg snorted.

"How'd you get caught this time?" Williams asked.

"I dunno," Nick mumbled, looking at the ground.

The officers exchanged glances. They knew Nick's uncle Robert as a violent drunk who had no qualms about coming after cops. There had been a fight involving him and a pool cue versus four cops three months earlier. The cops got revenge because he was resisting arrest, but none of the officers walked away without lumps. They weren't eager to tangle with him again over a boy. They also knew that their next call might be to pick up a bloodied mess of an eleven-year-old.

Hornburg sighed.

Williams turned to face Nick. He leaned down so they were closer to being eye to eye.

"You know what your uncle would do if we brought you home to him, don't you?" Williams said.

Nick nodded.

"If we ever catch you stealing again, you know that we'll have to tell him right? No matter what the consequences are for you."

Nick nodded.

"One warning."

Nick nodded.

"Then go."

Hornburg brought the bag and books out of his car. Nick grabbed them and ran off before the cops could change their minds.

Hornburg watched the boy run. "He might've killed that kid."

Williams sighed, got back in his car, and cranked up the stereo on his favorite rock station.

21 YEARS BEFORE THE CAPTAIN'S LAST SEASON

"I don't want to do this and neither do you," said Officer Williams. "You might not feel this way, but later on you will. I promise you that."

"Fuck you and what you think I'll think," Robert slurred.

Williams had been sent on a domestic violence call, which was all too common in Banff Park. It wasn't until he pulled up to the house that he realized it was Nick's. The door was open a few inches so he leaned into it with his shoulder, his hand on his pistol.

"Hello?" Williams had yelled. "It's the police. I'm coming in."

It had been a year since the shoplifting incident. He had all but pushed him out of his mind.

Robert was waiting for him in the kitchen. A lime green table separated the two men. Robert reached down and pulled out a crowbar that was on a kitchen chair.

Williams had wondered why on God's green earth there was a crowbar there to begin with. A cigarette dangled from Robert's lips and the smoke wafting up caused him to wince.

"Is anyone else here?" Williams had asked.

"Maybe there are, maybe there aren't." The cigarette bobbed in Robert's mouth while he talked.

Robert glared at Williams. He patted the crowbar with his free hand. Williams reached down and unbuckled the snap that held his service revolver in place.

"Whatcha going to do, piggy?" Robert yelled. "Shoot me for having a crowbar on my own damn property? In my own house?"

"I guess that depends on if you plan on using it or not. If I were you, I would put it down so that I can feel comfortable enough to take my hand off my gun, but that's up to you."

In his peripheral vision, Williams saw Nick. His face had been used as a punching bag and his left arm had an unnatural bend.

One shot was all that Nick remembered, and a flurry of police, ambulances and flashing lights. Policemen were asking him questions while two other guys were putting something on his throbbing arm.

That night Tom, Carol and Max came to visit Nick in the hospital. Max came into his room smiling and it made Nick mad, even though he didn't know why.

"Hey buddy," Tom said. "Are you all fixed up?"

"Yeah," Nick said, holding up his cast. "My arm itches and it's a little sore but I'm fine."

"Have you seen your aunt?" Carol asked.

"No, she ran off before the cops came," Nick responded.

"The Children's Protective Service is talking about putting you into a foster home." Carol couldn't get a read on Nick. He wasn't making eye contact and he kept adjusting the cup on his bedside table. Then she saw his chin quiver. "How about you stay with us instead?"

"For reals?" One of Nick's tears broke loose and ran down his face.

"Yeah, for reals," Max shouted. "Every night will be a slumber party."

"We'll pick your stuff up from your house and you can live with us," Tom said. "Is that okay?"

"That's so awesome," Nick said.

Nick never saw his aunt again.

20 YEARS BEFORE THE CAPTAIN'S LAST SEASON

Tom stood at the head of the table with Carol, Max, and Nick seated for dinner. It was his last dinner before leaving to captain his fishing vessel, the *Ms. Remorse*, for the first of three back-to-back crabbing seasons that would cover a four-month period for the crew, and including preparation and paperwork, a five-month period for the captain. Having a family meal before heading out to the Bering Sea was a ritual that Tom both loved and hated. He loved to be surrounded by his wife and sons, sharing great food and talking, but he hated that it would be the last time that he saw his family for a month - or, in the absolute worst case scenario, the last time he saw them. Out of the corner of his eye, he thought he could see Carol staring at him.

"Who wants to say grace?" Tom said. This was the only meal which Carol insisted that they say a blessing for.

"I think it would be nice if each of us said a little something," Carol responded. "Who would like to go first?"

After a moment of silence, with everyone looking at each other, Nick said, "I'll go first."

Tom nodded at Nick with a smile.

"Dear God," Nick said. "Thank you for this food and for the Staleys taking me in. Please let Tom have a safe trip and catch a lot of crab so he can come home early and watch Blackhawks games with us."

Nick stopped and opened his eyes. Max looked at him.

"Please let Dad not get seasick like he did that one year," Max said. "And have all the other men be safe, and not let the crab pinch their fingers."

"Also," Carol said, "Thank you for providing my family with food and a wonderful, safe home."

"Lord," Tom finished, "Please provide my wife and sons with safety and love in their hearts. In Jesus's name we pray, amen."

After dinner, the boys were sent to bed so they could be up early in the morning to say goodbye.

"It's your first time with the two boys all by yourself," Tom said.

"It should be fine," Carol said. "They're pretty good boys and they'll keep each other occupied. How's the crew looking?"

"I think we have a good one but you never can tell. Chuck, Mike, and the rest of the guys have all done this before, so at least I won't have to deal with a greenhorn this year."

Tom was lost in thought for a moment thinking about his crew, when he looked up at Carol.

"I wrote down the instructions for the snow-blower." He said.

"If it doesn't work, I have two boys who are perfectly capable of shoveling."

"Also, if it snows a lot, make sure the boys get on the roof and shovel that off as well."

"I know. I've done this plenty of times before."

"But not with two boys."

"It might be easier with two than with one. Max has a full-time play buddy and we have an extra hand around the house."

"So everything will be fine?"

"Yes. Everything will be fine."

"We go through this every time you leave," Carol replied. "You ask me a lot of questions about how we're going to manage without you. Meanwhile you're the one off doing the most dangerous job on earth. It always makes me feel like you're preparing me for you not coming back."

"I'm just concerned."

"I know you are. I'm ready for you to finish working on the boat."

"So am I. You know that."

"I'm ready for you to be back already."

"I'm ready to be back as well. We'll talk while I'm on the boat, and it will go a lot more quickly than we think."

"Fine. I'm still not happy about you leaving."

"Okay, love. I guess there isn't much I can do about that."

Some time after his parents went to bed, Max snuck into Nick's room.

"Nick," Max whispered. "Nick-o."

"Yeah," Nick said. "Where are you?"

"Down here."

Nick leaned over the side of his bed.

"What are you doing down there?"

"Laying down."

"Why?"

"Because."

"Okay."

"Dad's leaving tomorrow."

"I know. It sucks."

"What if something happens to him?"

"Nothing's going to happen. The captain's way tough. Nothing has happened before, right? Doesn't he go away every year?"

"Yeah, but every year is different."

"No way. Every year is the same. They do the same thing every time and your dad is the toughest guy we know. Do you ever see any weak guys with beards that awesome?"

"No, not really. His beard is awesome. Do you think he's tougher than your uncle?"

"My uncle wasn't tough. He was a dick. And he didn't have a cool beard."

"What do you mean?"

"Dicks aren't tough. If you kick them, they get hurt."

Max started laughing.

"Nick, I'm not sure that makes sense."

"Sure it does. Trust me. Let's get some rest so we can get up in the morning."

"All right. Do you mind if I sleep in here tonight?"

"Yeah, go ahead."

"Goodnight."

"Goodnight."

The next morning, Tom went into Max's room and couldn't find him. Then he went to Nick's room and saw his son sleeping on the floor. He hadn't ever thought about it before but he realized that, as an only child, Max must have been lonely sometimes. Tom knew that he couldn't have picked a better friend for his son to have.

"Time to get up, boys," Tom said, turning on the lights.

Max sat up, rubbing his eyes. Nick hid his head under the pillow, then peeked out with one eye, then both, to face the light.

"It's time for you to go already?" Max said.

"Yes," Tom sighed.

Max crawled up from the floor, wiped the spittle off the corner of his mouth and hugged his dad.

Nick got out of bed and went over to Tom. He didn't know if he should hug him or not until Tom pulled Nick close and embraced him.

"Be good," Tom said. "Okay?" He looked Nick in the eyes. Nick nodded yes.

"It's okay, Nick. It looks like I squeezed a few tears out of you."

Nick nodded again.

Tom put his hands on both of their shoulders. "Okay boys, I love you both and be good. If I hear about you misbehaving while I'm on the boat..." Tom stopped himself. He knew that he didn't need to make this speech.

Tom left the room. A few moments later, the boys heard Carol and Tom go out the front door. Both of them laid back down. Neither fell back asleep.

19 YEARS BEFORE THE CAPTAIN'S LAST SEASON

Nick was sitting at his desk trying to figure out his algebra homework. He didn't understand the need for quadratic equations, but whether he cared for them or not, he needed to pass the class. Doing well in school was a big deal in the Staley house. After his second year of living with his new family he was still adjusting to his new home. They bought him new clothes and he never had to worry about getting hit or whether the heat would be on. He felt like he had won the lottery.

"Hey pal," Tom said, standing in Nick's door. Tom looked around the bedroom and was surprised at how clean it was. He had never met a boy that took care of his stuff so well. "Do you want to take the little boat out on the Kenai River and do some fishing this weekend?"

"I don't have a fishing pole," Nick said, furrowing his eyebrows.

"Don't worry, we have plenty," Tom responded. "We'll slay those kings."

"Yeah we will," Nick said with his eyes lit up.

Carol sat in the front of the boat, the boys sat together in the middle and Tom was in the back, his hand on the throttle of the outboard motor.

"This looks like a good spot," Tom said as he dialed down the engine so that instead of moving up the river they stayed in one place.

"Nick, cast over there in the shade," Carol said. "That's where the big ones like to hang out."

Nick stood up and with his pole. "I'm not sure how."

Max cast his lure into the shade along the shoreline with barely any effort.

Carol took a graceful step and stood on the bench next to Nick.

"You just flip the line guide and hold the line against the pole," Carol said. "Then as you whip the rod, as you let go of the line and watch the lure fly."

Nick gave it a try. His first cast wasn't pretty, but it got the lure into the shade.

"Now reel in slowly," Carol continued. "A little quicker than that."

Nick's pole bent, went slack, and then bent towards the river violently.

"Don't let him drag you into the water, buddy," Tom said.

"First cast!" Max yelled with a little bit of jealousy. "Awesome."

"Okay now," Carol said. "Don't fight him or it will break the line."

Nick's line lurched up stream.

"He's going to go up river and then swim down using current to try to shake you," Carol continued. "Max, pull in your line so that you guys don't get tangled."

As if on command, the fish turned and swam down river. Nick reel whirred and he watched as his spool of line get smaller.

"When he stops it means that he is tired so you have to reel, reel, reel as fast as you can so that we can get him closer to the boat. Keep your pole up. Okay, now!"

The tension on his pole eased for a moment and Nick began to reel. He could feel the fish getting closer. In a flash the fish began to fight.

"Okay, let him fight it out."

The king salmon jumped and splashed a dozen yards from the boat. Tom picked up the net and handed it to Carol.

"Reel, reel, reel," she instructed.

As the fish came closer she dipped the net into the water and lifted the salmon. It wiggled for freedom as she dropped it into the boat.

The salmon flopped around with the silver Pixie lure hooked into its mouth.

"Here you go," Max handed Nick the small wooden bat.

"Whack him right on top of the head," Carol said.

Nick held it for a moment and then smacked the fish. He hit the fish again and its grills stopped moving in and out. Blood ran out of the fish's head.

"That's a little gross," Nick said.

"It sure is," Carol responded.

17 YEARS BEFORE THE CAPTAIN'S LAST SEASON

The bell rang and Max and Nick began to gather their books for third period when the teacher walked over and stood in front of the door.

"Sit down, sit down. The principal has an announcement," the teacher said. He went back to his desk and opened the sports section of the Anchorage Daily News.

Nick thought that the teacher had looked at him and Max in a weird way, but he wrote it off. He figured teachers must have something inherently wrong with them to subject themselves to high schoolers every day for little pay.

The principal's voice came on over the intercom. "Good morning Chugiak High. There have been reports of students using drugs in our school, and so in cooperation with the Anchorage Police Department, the school is officially on lockdown until locker searches are complete." Max glanced at Nick, who realized Max had pot in their shared locker.

The rest of the class began to joke about doing drugs and about who was definitely going to jail.

Max and Nick walked to the back of the classroom, away from their friends.

"Dude," Max said. "Dad is going to kill me."

"We can just say that it's mine," responded Nick.

"What?" Max was surprised. "No. Why?"

"You have good grades and shit. I'm an orphan. Your parents don't get as mad at me as they do at you."

"They're going to be pretty fucking mad at you too." Max wanted to talk Nick out of taking the rap, but he also knew that Nick had a point.

"I know. Either way we're in deep shit, so let me handle it, okay?"

Max didn't say anything as he tried to find the courage to stand up to Nick and tell him that he would handle it.

"You have to know that the cops will know if we are lying," Nick continued. "Cops are taught how to read people's faces. Trust me."

"All right," Max said. "We're so fucked."

The principal came back on over the intercom a few minutes later. "Please proceed to your fourth period class. Thank you for your cooperation."

Nick didn't know if it was luck of the draw because there were more than 1,500 lockers in the school, or if there were even drug dogs to begin with, but he didn't care. He dragged Max to the bathroom and made him flush the marijuana immediately. He was thankful that he didn't have to tell his adopted parents about the drugs. For the first time in his life, he had expectations to live up to.

15 YEARS BEFORE THE CAPTAIN'S LAST SEASON

Tom had grilled on the back deck and was admiring the view of the Sleeping Lady mountain with Nick after dinner.

"You boys are almost done with school," Tom said.

"Yep," Nick replied. "Not before we gave you a few extra gray hairs in your beard."

"Those are from crabbing. There wasn't ever a question about whether you guys were going to graduate." Tom said, rubbing his beard. "What are you going to do with yourself?"

"I thought I would work on the crab boat with you."

"You don't want to go to the university?"

"I don't really have the grades for it."

"The grades for UAA? I thought everyone got in."

"I guess they do, but I don't like school so why would I pay to go to one?"

"Because education provides for an easier life. And Carol and I will cover the cost."

Nick sat up straight in his chair. "That's very nice of you guys. You've already done more than I could ever ask for."

"You're like a son to us."

"You mean the good son?"

"I wouldn't go that far." They both chuckled.

"Instead of the university, why don't you learn how to weld or fix an engine? That way you'll have a trade and I could use you on the boat for more than labor."

"Okay. I'll look into it and see if I can find some classes."

Tom got up and went inside. He returned a short time later and tossed Nick a tabbed course catalog for the Stevens Technical College.

"Start at the blue tab," Tom said. "That's where all the fun stuff is."

14 YEARS BEFORE THE CAPTAIN'S LAST SEASON

Nick and Liz exited the movie theater, angling towards Round Table Pizza to meet up with some friends. Nick spotted Liz's ex-boyfriend Sean and two of his friends across the parking lot. It was bad enough that he had to sit through *Titanic*. To make matter worse, he didn't like Liz that much. She was cute, but all she wanted to talk about was *Friends* and *Melrose Place*, and Nick didn't care for either of them.

"Oh God," Liz said. "Those guys are such assholes."

"It's not a big deal," Nick said.

"Hey Nick," Sean yelled. "Who's the bitch?"

"Don't pay attention to them," Liz said to Nick, rolling her eyes. She started to walk quickly.

Nick didn't feel like getting in a fight – much less having to fight three guys at the same time. He took a deep breath and kept walking.

"I guess it's you," Sean said. His buddies laughed.

Nick knew these guys weren't going to let up. He decided that if he was going to be forced to fight, he might as well get in a shot or two.

"That's cute," Nick responded. "I can't imagine why Liz dumped your sorry ass."

Sean and his two buddies started walking towards them. Nick let go of Liz's hand and stood his ground. He popped his knuckles, turned his baseball cap backwards, and took a deep breath.

A maroon Astrovan squealed into the parking lot and Max, Chris and DJ jumped out. Chris had graduated a year earlier and had played offensive lineman, while his little brother DJ was a defensive lineman. Nick never felt comfortable around them, but Max liked them because they made him feel tough by association.

"Hey Sean," Max said with a smile. "Is there a problem?"

"It looks like there's a problem," Chris said, standing close to one of Sean's buddies. The guy's head only reached his chest.

"Nah, there's no problem," Sean said.

Nick went from being nervous about getting into a fight to being afraid for Sean and the other two guys.

DJ walked behind Sean and his friends, circling them like a predator.

"Are you sure there isn't a problem?" DJ said. "If there is I bet it wouldn't take long to fix it."

"It's cool." Sean and his friends walked towards their car, looking back a few times to make sure they weren't going to get jumped.

Chris put his huge arm around Liz's small shoulders and walking her toward the pizzeria. "See, everything is cool. Let's eat some pizza. I'm starving."

"Dude, you're almost three hundred pounds, you're always starving," DJ mumbled.

"That was fun," Max said as he walked over to Nick. "I got paid today, Nicky — my treat."

"Sweet," Nick said. His stomach hurt and he knew he wouldn't be able to eat.

12 YEARS BEFORE THE CAPTAIN'S LAST SEASON

Carol wondered around the house, rearranging items on the shelves and checking the clock every two minutes. For the first time in her marriage, she had the house all to herself.

Last year, Tom and Max had left to work on the boat while Nick stayed behind to finish school. The Ms. Remorse caught its quota of red king crab in three days and after taking the crab to the processors, they still had two weeks until the opilio season, so they were able to fly back to Anchorage for five days before heading back to prepare. More than a few times Tom had been stuck on the boat for the whole five months.

In order to finish the welding program before the next crabbing season, Nick had taken more than a regular load of classes. He had been gone most the day at school, but at least she could hear him come home at night and leave in the morning. Her house hadn't been totally empty.

The guys had only been gone for half an hour, and the lack of noise in her house was eerie. She turned on ESPN's Sportscenter without sitting down to watch it, but the theme song and excited cadence of the announcers was familiar and comforting.

Carol grabbed her book, a bodice-ripper that a friend wanted her to read, and thumbed through it. Then she sighed, went upstairs, and put on her workout clothes. She wanted to go for a walk but at 10 degrees, it was unseasonably cold, even by Eagle River standards.

She went to the garage and got on the treadmill. Trixie's replacement, Ron, also a female yellow lab, followed her out and curled up in the corner. Carol had tried to convince the guys to call her dog something else. She would have settled for any girl's name, but the more she argued against it, the more the name stuck.

After her workout she boiled a pot of water and dumped in a family-size box of pasta before realizing that she was only cooking for one. With the boys around, she could make enough for six people and the leftovers would disappear within a day or two, even if she didn't actually see anyone eat it. After she finished eating, she put the rest of the pasta into three plastic containers and tossed them into the fridge. She sighed. Her grandkids would come over later that day and she would just feed it to them.

When they arrived in Dutch Harbor, Nick was wide-eyed, trying to take it all in. It was the first time he had seen the boat up close. The men boarded the boat and descended into the galley.

"Here's your bunk," Max said. "Do you want the top or the bottom?"

"Top, I guess," Nick replied.

"Take the bottom," Tom yelled from the kitchen. "It doesn't sway as much when we're in rough seas."

"Bottom it is," Nick said, tossing his duffel bag on the bed. "Now what?"

"We get to work," Max responded with a smile. "But first we'll get a drink."

Tom, Nick and Max piled into cab that took them to the Brass Buckle, known in town as the Brass Knuckle.

As they walked through the door, Nick noticed a group of scowling, goateed men playing cards. The game stopped when the men turned around to see who came in.

Tom marched straight to the bar and slapped his hand on the wood while the two boys took a seat on stools.

"My son Nick will kick anyone's ass in this rinky-dink saloon," Tom announced. "And I'll put a hundred dollars down on it."

Nick smiled until he realized that Tom had laid down five twenty-dollar bills on the bar's smooth, water-ringed surface. The room went silent.

Then from the back, out of the shadows, an old man slowly rose, using a four-pronged walker to balance.

"I got your hundred right here," the old man said. His raspy voice betrayed a lifetime of smoking. Under his faded blue Alaska Aces baseball cap, the man's wrinkled face looked as if he had spent his whole life on the ocean, exposing his skin to the sun and its reflection off the water. His withered arms hung loose in his shirt sleeves, and he couldn't straighten his knees, but the brightness in his eyes showed spirit.

Nick looked the old man in the eye, hopped off his stool and shook out his hands.

"Whoa, Tiger," Tom said. Confused, Nick turned to look at him. "Holy crap boys, he was going to do it!"

Every man in the bar burst into hoarse, loud laughter. Nick blushed.

"I wasn't going to do it," Nick said. "I was just trying to scare him."

"You were too," Max said, with a grin. "Don't even try to pretend you weren't."

"Well," Nick said. "A hundred dollars is a lot of money."

"I would've dropped you like a bad habit, young man," the old fellow yelled as he lowered himself back into his seat.

"They did that to me last year," Max said.

"It's all fun and games until someone's grandpa gets his head knocked off." Nick sat back down on the stool and saw that the bartender had poured them three glasses of whiskey on the rocks.

Nick and Max looked at Tom.

"If I'm going to buy the booze," Tom said. "I get to decide what we drink. To the first season and the first time I've been to a bar with both of you guys. Cheers."

10 YEARS BEFORE THE CAPTAIN'S LAST SEASON

Nick pulled into Tom and Carol's driveway. He stopped for a moment and looked at the house. He loved how it looked illuminated with Christmas lights. The snow covered the lights and made the house look as if it were glowing.

He went into the trunk and pulled out a little present and stuffed it into his jacket pocket. Then he reached in, bent his knees, and lifted a big wrapped box. He couldn't see over it so he walked carefully up the few stairs, leaned over, and rang the doorbell with his elbow.

He heard the door open.

"Hello?" Nick said.

"Hi Nick," Carol said. "Come on in. You don't need to ring the doorbell. This is your home too."

"Thanks. I know. My hands are a little full."

"I can see that. Put it by the tree – I don't think it will fit under it – and come to the kitchen. We're having glogg."

"Okay," Nick stood still a moment. He couldn't tell if she had walked away or if she was still standing in front of him. After peeking around the side of the box, he went into the living room and set the gift down.

"The prodigal son returns," Max said from the recliner.

"Returns? I live a mile and a half down the road. You're jealous that I have my own apartment. I'm pretty sure that you're the prodigal son," Nick responded. "I'm the one they actually wanted. They chose me."

Max smiled. After eleven years, he still hadn't come up with a proper retort for that line.

"Why aren't you in the kitchen?" Nick asked.

"I thought I would give you your present real quick," Max said.

"You got me something? I thought we said that we weren't going to give gifts this year."

"Yeah, well..." Max picked a present off the side table and tossed it to Nick.

Nick reached into his jacket pocket and threw the box he had been hiding to a smiling Max.

"Same time?" Nick said.

"Yup," Max replied before ripping off the paper.

Nick opened his, laughed, and pulled out a bottle of whiskey. "I don't suppose you think I'm going to have to share this with you, right?"

"Maybe a little."

"I don't want to waste the good stuff on someone who won't appreciate it."

Nick held up the new fishing lures.

"We're going to tear them up this summer," Max said.

"Yeah buddy," Nick said. "We'll get our three silvers a day and spend the rest of the time drinking my whiskey."

"You're damn right," Max said.

Max didn't know if he should hug Nick or not so he stood and checked him with his shoulder instead. Nick pushed him back and they both laughed.

As they were going to the kitchen at the same time, Nick lunged and pushed Max into the door jamb. Max's shoulder shook part of the house, then Nick went through the door first.

"What was that?" Tom said.

"I don't know," Nick said. "I think Maxie fell or something."

Tom sighed and shook his head.

After dinner they all walked into the living room.

"What's in the big box, Nikko?" Tom said, picking it up. "Wow. That SOB is heavy."

"Yeah, don't hurt yourself old fella," Nick said.

"See Dad," Max said. "The reason why that's funny is because it's true. You're old. There's humor in truth."

"Honey," Tom asked Carol, "Is there any way that we can trade in these boys and adopt different ones? These two are defective."

"Tom, I think you should open that one first," Nick said.

"Yeah?" Tom responded. "The big boy? All right."

Tom pulled off the paper, revealing a TV box.

"What?" Max was confused. "You got them a TV?"

"No. Open it."

Tom opened the top and looked inside.

"Holy shit," Tom said. He looked at Carol. "Sorry."

"What is it?" Carol asked.

Tom reached down and pulled out the polished steel mermaid with conch shells over her breasts and wind-blown hair.

"I thought I could weld it to the front of the boat," Nick said. "If that would be okay with you."

"Did you make this?" Tom ran his hands over the scales of the mermaid's tail.

Carol put her hand over her heart and smiled.

"Yeah," Nick said. "I wish I would have made the hair a little longer."

"No. It's perfect. I would love to have this on the boat."

"Who knew?" Max said with a smile. "We have a friggin' artist in the family."

4 YEARS BEFORE THE CAPTAIN'S LAST SEASON

Nick sat on Max and Julie's couch, watching people interact at the party. He kept himself separate from everyone else, not because he thought he was better than them, or anyone else for that matter. He just wasn't socialized in the same way. It wasn't that he couldn't get along with them – he was clever and charming when he wanted to be – but all of the problems his peers had felt trivial to him.

Growing up, he had spent most of his day wondering if his uncle was going to kick his ass when he got home, so whether some young lady thought he was cute really didn't matter to him. Most of the time he didn't care to make the effort anymore.

Even though he was 29, the disconnect from his peers was still there.

Julie plopped down next to Nick on the couch so that they were connected at the jeans, hip to knee. Julie looked at him for a moment, then watched the party, trying to see what he was looking at.

"Hi Nick," she said, with a slight martini-fueled slur, brushing her bangs out of her eyes.

Nick looked at her. "Oh hi, Julie. I didn't notice you there."

Julie laughed a little. "So I don't get to talk to you very often even though you're my husband's best friend. You don't like me, do you?"

"Of course I do. I like you in spite of the fact that you stole my platonic life-partner."

"He might have been happier if he married you."

"Nah," Nick said. "I'm horrible in bed."

"Do you think I'm mad at you because you banged two of my friends and didn't call either of them back? I'm not mad. I think it was a little shitty though."

Nick had wondered if she was ever going to bring it up. It had been a few years ago. Now she finally had enough liquid courage to call him out. "Yeah, it was pretty shitty. I didn't mean to get you involved. I apologize."

"It's okay. I mean, I only had to listen to each of them whine about you for a little while. I guess I have to forgive you because my husband loves you so much."

"Well, he has always found me cute."

"You know what I mean. Don't be weird. It's okay. Seriously, it's cool. We both know that if he needed your kidney, you would give it to him."

"He doesn't want my kidneys. He would be worse off."

"That's probably true. I don't know though. I'm going to tend to my party." Julie got off the couch. "Happy St. Patrick's Day. Go mingle around, meet some people."

"I will." Nick had no intention of mingling.

"You lie," Julie said, pointing at him and glaring. Then her glare broke into a smile and she walked away.

Nick went into the kitchen to get another beer where a small group of people was handing out shots. A short, good-looking blonde grabbed his arm and pulled him into the circle.

"Do you want a shot of ver, veerstu?" she said. Her bright blue Scandinavian eyes could have made him do anything .

"I think it's called tequila," Nick responded. "With a T, not a V."

"Yeah. Vequila."

"Sure. I'll have a shot. Are you sure you need another?"

She nodded and stumbled forward a little, as though her head were full of fluid and she was fighting the waves.

Once everyone had a shot glass, someone in the crowd yelled, "To Ireland."

They raised the glasses in a toast. Most of them touched the bottoms of their glasses to a table or a counter in an unknown ritual that they felt the need to follow. Nick didn't bother. There was no reason for the shot to take a longer route to his stomach.

The tequila warmed him as it went down. He felt his cheeks flush for a few moments and then saw Max come down the stairs that ran adjacent to the kitchen.

"Staying out of trouble?" Max asked.

"Yeah, but not for long," Nick said with a smirk. Then he nodded in the direction of the blonde.

"Dude." Max suddenly became serious. "Are you kidding? Julie still hasn't forgiven you for humping her other friends."

"Sure she has," Nick responded, maintaining his grin. "She just told me that she did."

"I'm not sure that applies to her cousin though."

"Crap."

"Crap is right."

"All right." Nick knew that if he stayed, Julie would end up mad at him. "That's my cue to leave."

"You should crash here for the night."

"I think some distance between me and her cousin is a good idea for the both of us."

"My marriage thanks you."

They shook hands and Nick left.

Nick had hoped to get home before the heavy snow flurries started but it was too late. The next thing he knew, the car was turning and there was nothing he could do to stop it. Nick had thought that people who told stories about their significant life experiences occurring in slow motion were full of shit. He now knew it was true.

All the directions he knew for controlling a car sliding on ice were for mitigating damage over a long distance. He needed to stop instantly. The soft thump that he heard on the back left panel of his car betrayed how much his life was going to change.

He knew he had enough alcohol on his breath that when his car finally came to a stop, he was headed to jail. Any amount is too much when a kid is hit by a car, even if it is the kid's fault.

After getting his car under control, Nick stopped and got out. He looked to his left and saw a sledding hill with tracks leading into the road. For a moment he got mad that kids were dumb enough to sled into the street at night. He wondered what kind of parents would allow that.

A man ran down the hill wailing, "No no no no no." Nick also began to jog over to the little girl gasping in the middle of the road. Houses' outside lights turned on. People silhouetted in their windows looked out to the street and a few people came out.

The man who ran down the hill was holding the little girl. He put her down and came at Nick. If there was one thing Nick knew, it was when a man was going to try to hurt him. Every man that had ever had bad intentions for him had the same look in his eyes.

The guy was a typical suburban softie, and if Nick had timed it right, he could've sprung off the ball of his right foot, taken a big step with his left and threw a right-handed haymaker to stop the guy in his tracks. But he didn't. The man got close to him and started throwing punches that Nick didn't try to evade. He held up his arms to protect his head. Nick slipped on the ice and the man landed on top of him. The man threw punch after punch through his tears until he lost control and tried to pound Nick like a nail into the ground. Some of the men from the neighborhood pulled him off.

Nick stayed on the ground. Even though four men were holding onto him, the man almost broke free and came back for another round. No one came over to see if Nick was okay, but he didn't blame them.

While he was debating whether he should get up or not, he heard a siren. He put his head back down and stayed still. He could feel blood running out of his nose and down the sides of his face. Ever since he had his nose broken when he was six, it took barely more than a stiff breeze to start the blood flow.

A police cruiser arrived with an ambulance close behind, the sirens deadened by the snow. He walked over to his car and turned it off. Blood from his nose dripped down the back of his throat. He walked over to the police cruiser and leaned against it. The cop was talking to some of the neighborhood folks who must have mentioned Nick, because they all turned and looked at him at the same time. He blushed. Even though it had been an accident, he had plenty to be ashamed of. Nick watched the EMTs put the girl on a child-size spinal board. It made him sad to think that there was ever a need for the little board.

Nick thought about his car's speed and the way he had hit the girl. He wondered if she could possibly survive.

The officer strolled over to Nick. They were the same height, but the officer was doing his best to project himself as taller. He puffed his chest out until he got closer and saw Nick's busted-up face in the dim streetlight.

"What happened to you?" said the cop. He had the last name Johnson on his uniform.

"I think that guy's her father," Nick said, nodding at the man climbing into the ambulance. "He got after me a bit."

"You look like shit," Officer Johnson said. "Do you want to press charges?"

"No." Nick sighed and watched the ambulance drive away.

"Have you had anything to drink tonight?"

Nick wanted to lie but he knew that the cops would give him a Breathalyzer no matter his response. "Yep. A few."

"How many is a few?"

"Three or four. I don't know."

"Okay." The cop opened the back door, then turned to Nick. "Do we need cuffs? I would rather we didn't because it looks like you have had enough rough stuff for the night."

"It's fine, officer. I've made enough bad decisions for one night."

"All right. Hop in back and we can go from there. Watch your head."

Nick was glad he didn't put the cuffs on him. It was bad enough sitting in the back of the car while the lights were on. He sighed at his own conceit. He couldn't believe that he was thinking about being embarrassed after he had probably just killed a child. He started to do the mental math about his jail time, trying to steel himself for the worst. Manslaughter was going to carry at least a five-year stretch at Spring Creek Correctional Facility in Seward, including time off for good behavior. For the rest of the ride, he stuffed down his emotions and calculated the consequences of his actions.

Two officers were waiting for them at the station. The cops from Anchorage were sending out a crime-scene investigation unit, but it wouldn't take a scientist to figure out what had happened.

A young cop approached Nick and Officer Johnson.

"No cuffs?" he sneered. "Jesus. What did you do? His face looks like he was resisting arrest."

"Screw off Blanchfield," said Johnson. "He was like that when I picked him up."

"Sure he was," said Blanchfield with a smile.

The district commander approached as the cop led Nick to his holding cell.

"Nick, it's been a while."

"Yes it has, Officer Williams. I had hoped that it would be longer."

"You and me both, son."

Neither of them reached to shake hands. Johnson looked at them, expecting an explanation, but neither offered one.

Seeing Nick in his station made Williams melancholy. He knew that Nick would have to pay for this bad decision for the rest of his life.

"Take him back to Room 4," Williams ordered.

Johnson put Nick in the last room on the left. There were two chairs on one side of a short metal table and one chair on the other.

Nick sat down and put both elbows on the table, with his fingertips together in a steeple fashion. Then he leaned his forehead against his thumbs. For the first time since the accident he was alone. He started to cry for the girl and for himself. He had ruined two lives.

3 AND A HALF YEARS BEFORE THE CAPTAIN'S LAST SEASON

A cop brought Nick into the courtroom in handcuffs. Nick thought the courtroom appeared to be designed by the people who produced Holiday Inns. Two drab desks for the prosecution and defense, with a patterned carpet straight out of a John Hughes movie. He wished that the place that was going to send him to prison looked a little more grandiose.

Max thought that his adopted brother looked like shit after only a few months in jail. Nick's hair was greasy and he needed to shave. Max was frustrated because Nick had always planned to plead guilty, but the overworked judicial system took its time processing him.

Although both sides knew that Nick was going to go to jail, they disagreed about the length of the term.

The grieving parents thought that five years wasn't enough for the loss of their daughter, and had pressed for a longer term. Nick didn't blame them one bit.

Nick sat behind the desk next to his lawyer. He wore a black suit and blue tie that Max picked up for him at J.C. Penney. Alaska law dictated that as a person accused of a felony, he had to wear handcuffs connected to a chain around his waist. The chain limited his reach to less than a foot away from his stomach.

Nick wanted a drink from his glass of water but thought he would spill it on himself. That wasn't the impression he was aiming for right before he was sentenced.

Max, Tom, and Carol sat behind him, with Carol in the middle. Nick had requested that Julie stay home with the kids because he didn't want them to have to get a sitter because of him. The courtroom was no place for children.

An aisle divided the courtroom in half. The other side was filled with the family and friends of the girl Nick had hit and killed.

Kelly's parents and brother gave their impact statements to the judge. They told the judge how Kelly had been a sweet and smart girl. How she would never get married or have children. How everyone in the neighborhood knew who she was because she sold Girl Scout cookies from door to door. How her little brother cried for his sister every night. They told the judge how Nick had decimated their lives.

Nick held eye contact with all of the speakers no matter how many tears ran down his face. With his arms chained, he couldn't wipe his eyes.

When the family members finished speaking, the judge was quiet for a moment.

"Do you have anything to say for yourself, Mr. Ferris?" the judge asked Nick.

Nick took a deep breath. His lawyer had told him that it would be better if he kept his mouth shut, but he had to say something. Nick was the one who had to live with his actions, not his lawyer.

"Yes," he said. He cleared his throat and looked at Kelly's parents. "I know that there's nothing I can say to bring your daughter back. I'm truly sorry."

"That being said," the judge responded, "we'll adjourn while I make my decision." He banged his gavel and left the room.

2 YEARS BEFORE THE CAPTAIN'S LAST SEASON

"Sign here," said the obese lady guard in the waiting room. "I need ID."

Max didn't want to be there but, he thought, neither did Nick, so it was the least he could do.

The visit took a lot of planning. Early into his three-and-a-half year sentence Nick had been moved to Arizona because of overcrowding at the jails in Alaska. Max had wanted to visit for the past two years, but Nick wouldn't commit to a date. Finally Max set up his visitation, bought a plane ticket, and told Nick he was coming three days before he showed up.

He had given Nick a little money to buy some stuff from the commissary, even though Nick never asked him for it. Max didn't tell him that he had put money in his account until after it was done.

"Here you go," the guard said, handing him his driver's license. "Please take a seat."

"Thanks," Max said.

Max was the only adult male in the waiting room. The rest of the visitors were women and children. He took a seat in a hard, green plastic chair. Leaning back in the chair wasn't possible because of its convex egg shape, so he sat forward with his elbows on his knees. The Department of Corrections clearly didn't want visitors to get comfortable while they waited. On the table next to his chair someone had scrawled "ASSHOLE" with a pen and then ran over the letters repeatedly. It looked to him like they must have been in the waiting room for at least a week straight to get the grooves that deep. It didn't bode well for his potential wait.

A pale green cage surrounded the TV on the wall, with an opening around the screen. The TV was showing a 24-hour news station that repeated its broadcasts every thirty minutes. Tragedy, murder, scandal, and a feel-good story on an endless loop.

Halfway through Max's second run of the show, a beefy guard yelled out, "Max Staley."

Max stood and approached the guard who was holding a clipboard.

"That's me," Max said and then immediately realized that it wasn't necessary because he was the only male in the room and he had approached after the guy called out his name.

"ID?" he responded.

Max handed him his license. The guard compared it with the name on the clipboard and then gave it back.

"One in," the guard yelled.

There was a buzzing and the institutional gray bars slid open.

"Please step in and wait," the guard barked. "They'll let you through the second door once they shut this one. Don't touch the gates."

"Okay."

Max stepped in. The door behind him buzzed and then shut. For a moment Max felt claustrophobic. If they had decided to keep him in between the two doors, he wouldn't have been able to do anything.

Before he had a chance to freak out, the second door buzzed and opened. He stepped through. He was glad to be out of the small prison until he realized that there were now two doors between him and his freedom instead of one.

The guard on the other side said, "All the way down, on your left."

Max walked down a hallway and turned left. He had expected a big pane of bullet-proof glass and telephones like he had seen in movies. Instead, he saw a cafeteria with a bunch of circular tables and seats surrounding them. All the furniture was bolted to the ground.

Max stepped through the doorway. He heard someone say, "Hey pretty boy."

Max turned and saw Nick wearing a big smile. They shook hands and hugged, keeping their right arms between them.

When they pulled away, Max could see the fading yellow-green of a healing black eye.

Nick said, "Don't ask."

"Okay." For the first time since Nick went to prison, Max was scared for his friend. Nick was the toughest guy that Max had ever met, but it was obvious that everyone in jail was the toughest to someone, somewhere. "There has to be someone who can do something to help you."

"It doesn't work that way," Nick said. "How are the kids?"

"The boys are great," Max responded, taking his cue to drop it. Nick looked like he hadn't slept in days. Max stayed focused on his eyes, afraid to notice any other signs of deterioration. "Julie says hi."

"Yeah, tell her I appreciate the letters and the money. You don't need to do that, you know."

"I know. Thanks for writing the boys."

"Do they know where I am?"

"They know you are in Arizona."

"Do they know that I'm in jail?"

"Of course not."

"Good. Can we keep it that way?"

"That's the plan."

"Thanks."

"What's going on with you?" Max wanted to turn the conversation back to Nick because he was there to see how his friend was, not to talk about hiding the truth from his children. Talking about his life felt selfish, like he was rubbing his freedom in his friend's face.

Nick held his hands palms up and shrugged.

"I'm in prison. There really isn't much to tell."

"What do you do all day?"

"I sweep and clean the gym. Eat shitty food three times a day, and try not piss anyone off. How was the crabbing season?"

"It was decent. The Fish and Game changed the red king crab season to two weeks in November, which means we have more time to meet our quota but now we have to go out later in the year."

"No shit?" Nick said, shaking his head. "Now we'll have to go out when it's even colder?"

"Yeah, it's ridiculous. Four months of freezing our balls off. We'll still have to get lucky to earn a week or two off."

"If the weather cooperates."

"Exactly. The weather was so bad last year we weren't able to fly back to Anchorage for a week with the family. We were stuck on the island. We would've been better off in here."

"Not quite."

"Sorry. You know what I mean."

They spoke for the rest of the hour about sports and anything else unrelated to the fact that Nick was in jail.

Max flew home the next day. A week later, he wasn't surprised when he received a letter from Nick thanking him for his visit and asking him not to come back. Nick wrote that it was too hard to see his friend when he was locked up. He also mentioned the cost that Max must have put out to fly down and stay in a hotel room. Nick said that he had enough guilt on his plate. At the end of the letter, he told him that he loved him and his family and that he couldn't wait to see them when he was on the outside. It was the only time Nick had ever told Max that he loved him.

1 AND A HALF YEARS BEFORE THE CAPTAIN'S LAST SEASON

The prison yard wasn't much of a yard at all. It was a hundred yards by thirty yards of dirt and patches of weeds with a basketball court in the center.

Nick was furious about spending his 31st birthday behind bars. He didn't even want to have some celebratory wild night on the town. A dinner at Max's with his family would've been perfect.

He wanted to join the basketball game, but with a year left on his sentence, he had stopped playing because the games often got heated and he didn't want to risk more time by getting in a fight.

He was watching the game when the only other guy from Eagle River in the jail came and stood near him. Even though they were from the same small town, Nick knew Jesse was quick to fight and he didn't want to acknowledge him.

"Did you hear that son of a bitch Williams got cancers?" Jesse said.

"It's cancer," Nick said. "Singular, not plural."

"Then why is in multiple places then?"

Nick didn't care to engage Jesse in a conversation about grammar. He was surprised, but he didn't know if Jesse was telling the truth or not. In jail, half of the stories were about bad things happening to the people who had put them there.

"Oh yeah?" Nick said, continuing to watch the game.

"Yeah. My brother saw that they were doing a fundraiser for him in the *Alaska Star*."

The thought of one of Jesse's relatives reading the local paper furthered Nick's disbelief.

"Nice." Nick decided that once rec time was over he would write Max a letter and ask him about it.

That night Nick laid on his bunk and stared at the bunk above him. He wanted to help out Williams, but he didn't know how. He knew that Eagle River was small enough that the community would be able to pull together a fundraiser. He also knew that it wouldn't be enough.

6 MONTHS BEFORE THE CAPTAIN'S LAST SEASON

Max woke up before the rest of his family and started to make breakfast. He only worked five months a year, a fact that his wife liked to remind him of when he was neglecting his chores around the house. The rest of the year he worked short-term construction jobs. He was coming to the end of his crabbing hiatus. He dreaded going back onto the boat, but it was his dad's boat and eventually he would inherit it, just like his father had. He had spoken to Julie about selling the boat once his father died many times. He didn't want to get rid of the boat but he also didn't want his two sons growing up without him for part of the year. The only problem was that by the time his dad passed away, his boys would be grown up.

His father had told him that missing out on some events was the price he had to pay, but that wasn't enough for Max. Max's plan was to sell the boat and pick up another job in town. Combined with Julie's work as an accountant, the sale would put him and Julie in the black for the rest of their lives. He tried not to think about it. In the meantime, his kids were getting bigger by the day.

He made scrambled eggs and toast for the boys. He poured some coffee with a splash of milk for Julie.

He went upstairs into the master bedroom.

"Wake up buttercup." He touched Julie's bare arm. "Your coffee is next to the bed."

"I don't wanna get up," Julie said. She had a few glasses of wine before bed.

"I know. Only two more days until the weekend. Then we should go up to Denali or something with the boys. I'll make hotel reservations today."

Julie loved the national park but hated camping. She claimed that it was too dirty and she thought she heard bears wandering through camp all night.

In the weeks before he left to go on the boat, Max tried to bend over backwards to make sure that she knew how much he loved her because he didn't know if he would be coming back. He tried not to admit that was the only reason that he was being nice to his wife, but inside he knew it was pretty high up on the list.

She rolled over and smiled at him. "Okay. Yeah."

Even though he was absent for part of the year, he was a better husband than all of her friends' husbands combined.

He went into the boys' room.

"Rise and shine cowboys," he said, but inside he didn't want to wake them up. He wanted to watch them sleep.

Madden spun around in his bed, already awake. Even for a six-year old he was a bundle of energy. "I'm already shining Daddy!"

Tyler grunted and turned away from his father. At four and a half he had already taken on some his mother's traits. Even though they were close in age, the boys weren't alike at all.

Madden jumped off his bed and Max had to catch him. Julie hated when Madden jumped off the bed so Max automatically turned around and looked at the door to see if she was watching. "Don't do that around your mom, Maddy."

"I know because when she sees me, she gets like this." He made a scary face and curled his hands into claws.

Max started to laugh. "Don't let her see you do that either."

"She already saw," he said with a twinkle in his eye. "I had corner time."

Max couldn't help but smile. He didn't want to encourage him, but he couldn't contain his amusement. He went over to Tyler's bed, picked him up and tossed him over his shoulder. He scooped up Madden and carried him like a football. Madden pretended that he was Superman with his little arms and legs outstretched parallel to the ground.

When the three of them got to the kitchen, Julie was leaning over into the refrigerator, getting some fruit. She wasn't a breakfast person. Max put Madden down and set Tyler, who was still fighting through the fog of sleep, into one of the chairs. Madden ran and smacked his bent-over mom on the butt with a pop.

"Good morning Momma!" Madden yelled.

Max didn't know if she was going to be pissed or amused so he turned away and started putting the boys' breakfast on plates.

Julie turned around, saw her boy and smiled.

"Look what you've taught him to do," she said to Max.

"I have no idea what you are talking about," Max said, refusing to make eye contact. "Breakfast is ready."

Julie and Madden sat down at the table with Tyler. "Hi Mom," Tyler said with a little wave.

"Hi son," Julie said. Tyler's hair stuck up in the back like a peacock tail and it never failed to make her smile.

All three of the boys had eggs, toast, and fruit while Julie drank her coffee and had some toast. Max avoided caffeine until he was on the boat because when he got to work he wanted the full pick-me-up effect.

"So Nick is getting out next week," Julie said to Max. She said with a slight upturn in her voice at the end like it was a question, but it wasn't.

"Uncle Nick?" Madden said. Madden only had vague memories of Nick but he had received a letter or two a month from Nick while he was "vacationing in Arizona."

Before Max had a chance to respond, Julie sighed.

"Yes, Uncle Nick is coming for a visit," Max said.

"How long is he going to be staying with us?" Julie asked him as if they hadn't talked about it five or six times before. "I can't believe I'm going to have a 33-year-old ex-con under my roof," she said.

"What's an ex-con?" Madden said.

"Just a few days," Max said. "Then he's going to make other arrangements. Julie, you know he isn't a bad guy."

"Yeah, well tell that to Rachel or Neda," Julie responded. "Even if we look past the fact that he's been in jail for three-and-a-half years." They were heading down the same path that they always were when it came to Nick.

"He isn't a bad guy," Max said in a calm voice. He didn't want to get her upset or let the kids see them fight.

"It isn't that I don't like him as a person. I'm sure he'll be great with the kids. It's just that trouble follows him like a shadow."

Even when it came to his own wife, Max felt the need to stand up for Nick because beyond his family, no one else ever did.

"He's always been nice to you. He's family."

"I have to get ready for work." Julie got up from the table and went upstairs to shower.

"Uncle Nick was in jail?" Madden asked in a whisper after watching his mom leave.

"Yes, well, no. I don't know. Eat your breakfast or you're going to be late for school," Max said. He got up and started to clean the dishes while the boys finished their meal in silence.

Max drove two and a half hours south from Anchorage to Seward's Spring Creek Correctional Center. Nick had been flown back to Alaska with three months left in his term because the last portion of an inmate's sentence was to be served in his home state to help him get re-acclimated.

It was going to be strange having Nick around, even though it wouldn't be for long. Max was excited but equally apprehensive about seeing his friend. He hoped that Nick hadn't completely changed. Max realized that he had changed as well. He had two growing boys and all the responsibilities that come with having a family.

Max pulled into the parking lot and looked at the main entrance, two glass doors leading to what looked like a large A-frame house. Beyond the house was a tall watchtower that could be used for air traffic control. Around the perimeter of the facility stood two twenty-foot high fences, separated by ten feet, with three rolls of concertina wire coiled on top. One coil was on the inside of the fence, one was on top and the other was on the outside. It seemed like overkill to Max because the surrounding area was all but uninhabitable. There was frigid water on one side and steep mountains that extended for countless miles on the other. No one had ever escaped from the prison.

The doors opened and Nick walked out toward Max. He was wearing the same suit that he went in with three and a half years before. His tie dangled untied around his neck.

Max got out of the car and took a few steps toward him. They shook hands and then hugged with their other arms, keeping enough space between them to maintain their heterosexual status.

"Congrats on being out," Max said. He had thought about what he was going to say to Nick for days and that was all that he could come up with. He didn't have experience with picking people up from jail.

"Thanks for coming to get me," Nick said. "I'm not sure what to say."

"Of course," Max responded. "Do you want to go get something to eat? I'm starving."

"Hell ya. How about some Lucky Wishbone?"

"Three and half years of cafeteria food and you want a burger? Let's get some steak. Julie has the boys at home so we should have time to get something good to eat."

"It was a long time."

"Yes, it was."

They drove for a few minutes in silence.

"I know you want to ask, so just do it," Nick said.

"What are you talking about?" Max replied. He wasn't doing a very good job of holding back his smile.

"You don't know what I mean?" Nick said, looking at Max with accusation in his eyes.

"Nope." Max couldn't hold back his smile anymore.

"Fucker. There wasn't any man-on-man action, at least involving me. In case you are wondering," Nick growled.

"Oh my," Max chuckled, putting his right hand over his heart. "I didn't even think of that."

"You're an asshole."

"Does that mean you want to kiss me? That sounds like prison pillow talk."

Nick laughed.

They drove the two hours back, mainly talking about Max's life. Nick grilled him about the boys, and the boat and crew. Max thought talking about his normal life would bore Nick, but instead he listened as if he hadn't heard anything so interesting in his life.

Once in Anchorage, they went downtown and pulled into the parking lot of Sterling's Steakhouse.

"How's this?" Max said.

"Perfect," Nick said beaming.

After Nick's first post-prison meal, the guys stopped by the grocery store before heading home. Nick needed to pick up a few personal items. He left everything that he had acquired in the prison because he didn't want anything to remind him of where he had been.

They walked in the house. The boys and Julie were waiting in the living room. She had made bruschetta, and there was an open bottle of wine on the table.

Nick pulled out the flowers that he had been hiding behind his back.

"For you," Nick said, blushing a little.

"That's very kind of you, Nick," Julie smiled and turned to Max. "See what a gentleman does?"

Max laughed. "Yeah, but he hasn't seen a woman in three years."

"Three and a half," he chimed in. "I sat in jail for six months before the sentencing and it counted as time served."

"Boys, come say hi to your Uncle Nick," Julie said.

The boys got up and came over. Madden stood a little behind his mother. Tyler hugged her leg while peeking out from behind her with one eye.

"Say hi," Max said.

Both boys mumbled an almost inaudible version of hi.

"Hi guys," Nick said, getting down on one knee so that he was closer to being eye to eye with them. "I brought you something."

"Something from your trip?" Madden said.

"Yes," Nick pulled out foot-long toy trucks for both of them. "Do you like trucks?"

The boys nodded yes. Nick held them out and they tentatively came over and took them. Then they ran off to the living room to play with their new toys.

"Is that the end of bribing my family?" Max said. "Where's my gift?"

"Your gift is my eternal gratitude," Nick responded. "Isn't that enough?"

"I guess that work, but cash is always appreciated," Max smiled. "Let's take your stuff upstairs. You'll be sharing a bathroom with the boys. I hope you don't mind."

"I've been sharing a shower area with murderers. It'll be fine."

"You're less likely to get stabbed in here but much more likely to stub your toe on a toy in the bathtub."

"I'll take that exchange any day of the week."

They went into the guest bedroom where Nick's clothes were folded in piles on the bed, along with a new suitcase and matching backpack.

"We got your stuff from your place and kept it in the attic after you went to jail. We got your clothes and washed them so that you'd have something to wear."

"Thank you," Nick said, all of sudden feeling embarrassed at all that Max and Julie had done for him. "Mind if I take a shower?"

"Take your time." Max left the room, closing the door behind him.

Nick grabbed a handful of clothes and smelled them. He hadn't smelled anything that wonderful in years.

He turned on the bathtub faucet and couldn't figure out how to start the shower function. He was worried that he was going to have to ask for help until he pulled down on the handle and the shower began to flow.

He got in the shower and let the water cover him. He washed himself from head to toe three times, relishing that there wasn't a time limit or anyone waiting for him to exit.

5 MONTHS AND 27 DAYS BEFORE THE
CAPTAIN'S LAST SEASON

Max's phone rang. He knew it was Nick because he was the only one with the ringtone of Metallica's "Fade to Black."

"Hey man," Max said.

"Can you take me to the airport in the morning?"

"I'm great, thanks for asking," Max responded. "Yeah, sure. Where are you? What's up?"

"I got up early and didn't have anything to do so I took the bus to Lowe's and I'm looking at welding helmets. I have to go down to New Mexico to check on my grandmother," Nick said. "I haven't seen her in a while and the last time I talked to her she sounded a little out of it. I think she might have to go into a home or something."

"You have a grandmother?" Max didn't remember Nick mentioning her.

"Dude, everyone has a grandmother."

"I know, I haven't heard you talk about her before, and I've only known you twenty-five years and am your adopted brother. Is there anything else?"

In all of the years that he had known Nick, Max had only interacted with his aunt and uncle once. It was easy to forget that he had other family.

"No. I don't really know her either," Nick said. "You know my aunt hates her family and everyone else for that matter. I mean, I haven't talked to her very much. No one else in my family seems to give a shit so I might as well make sure she's okay. I could use a little time away from Alaska."

"All right. What time do we need to leave?"

"6:30 should be early enough."

"Yikes. I'll see you then."

Nick hung up without saying goodbye.

Max looked at the phone, saw that the call had ended and mumbled "Jerk" to himself at the exact moment that Julie walked into the room. She turned her head sideways.

"Was that at me?" She wasn't mad, just confused.

"Oh. No," Max smiled. "That was aimed at Nick."

Julie sat next to him. "Trouble in paradise, my love?"

"I'm taking Nick to the airport in the morning."

"Where is he off to? I didn't think he ever left your side."

"He's going to New Mexico to visit his grandma."

"It's strange to think that he has other family. I thought he had cut off all contact with them."

"Yeah, me too." Max didn't want to talk about it anymore. He was confused about why his friend had been holding back from telling him about his grandmother. "Want some wine?"

"Sure."

Max went to the kitchen.

5 WEEKS BEFORE THE CAPTAIN'S LAST SEASON

"I think there is someone at the door," Nick's grandmother called from her post on the couch.

"Okay," Nick said, grabbing a Santa Fe Pale Ale from the fridge.

He walked over and looked through the window next to the door. After robbing the bank he was worried about someone recognizing him. The police's composite picture, combined with the video footage from the bank, looked a lot like him. And the cops had run a picture of what he would look like without a beard. It was a little off, but not much.

He put on his cowboy hat before answering the door.

"It's $16.99," said the delivery guy in his blue and red uniform. Nick was happy to see that he, like most delivery guys, didn't make eye contact because he was most concerned about getting the money and moving on.

Nick nodded and handed him a $20 bill that he had already pulled out of his pocket. He wanted the interaction to be as short as possible.

"Who is it?" yelled his grandma.

"Keep the change," Nick said. He wanted to give a good tip, but not enough for him to be memorable. He went back inside.

"Pizza? I didn't know you liked pizza," his grandma said.

Nick wanted to say something about how he had ordered it three different times (from three different restaurants) and that she had eaten it with him each time, but when a person's mental capacities are slipping, there isn't a reason to point it out.

"Who doesn't like pizza, Grandma?" he said, trying to be as pleasant as he could.

"Your father liked pizza," she said.

"Really?" Nick didn't much about his dad. Mostly that when his father went for smokes, he didn't come back. His aunt Amy was his mother's sister and for some unexplained reason, she hated his father. No matter how many questions he asked, she wouldn't talk about him.

"Oh yes. He was a strapping young man," his grandma said. "Good looking too. When your mother first brought him home, I was a little worried for her."

"Worried?"

"Of course. Men like that can make women fall in love with no effort at all, and she was head over heels from the moment they made eye contact."

"But you liked him?"

"Everyone liked him besides Amy, and that was only because she was in love with him too. It was hard for Angela to deal with. When he came into a room, his smile would bounce all over. Even your grandfather liked him, and he didn't like anyone."

"When did you first meet him?" Nick was leaning forward on the couch. Then his grandmother's face went slack.

"When did I first meet who?" Her eyes were blank. The spark firing the memories had gone out.

"My dad," Nick said, hoping to pull her focus back.

"Who is your dad?"

"Geoff."

"Oh. Geoff? I don't know a Geoff." She started watching *The Price Is Right*.

Nick wanted to grab her shoulders and shake the memories out of her. He wanted to yell. The window on finding out about his father was getting smaller by the day. He hoped it hadn't closed forever.

3 WEEKS BEFORE THE CAPTAIN'S LAST SEASON

The captain and his wife were sitting at a table overlooking the ocean at a restaurant in La Jolla. The wealthy community in the northern part of San Diego had always made Tom a little uncomfortable because he came from a long line of fishermen and the people of La Jolla were doctors and lawyers. But he loved his wife and she wanted to go, so he did. They had honeymooned in San Diego almost forty years ago and each time they visited, Tom was amazed at how much the city had changed. Only the sea lions didn't change. They were still fat and sassy.

Tom had always loved the city's little beaches surrounded by sharp cliffs. There was a vast expanse of beach north of where they were sitting, but it didn't have the intimacy of the little coves that dotted the coast.

He still couldn't believe that his wife had stuck by him for all these years. It was easy to vow to stay with someone forever - people did it all the time - but hard to actually pull it off. None of the other fishermen his age had been able to hold on to their wives. He had been gone during different crabbing seasons since they met. She raised their son and Nick by herself while he was gone and she had done a good job. Max was a momma's boy (at least much more than Tom ever was) but that was to be expected of an only child.

Sitting at the table, Tom had a hard time not thinking about his dream from the night before. He was trapped in never-ending storm while his boat took a pounding. The metal hull was bending and flexing, roaring in his ears. A rogue wave burst through the window of the pilothouse and threw him out of his captain's chair. He got up and struggled to regain control of the boat as the wind and sleet blew in while Madden and Tyler sat on the bow of the boat, their toes dipping into the water during the troughs of the big waves. The boys shouted, "Wheeee..." with every wave. He woke up when he heard himself say, "Mayday, mayday, mayday..." The dream felt so real when he awoke he was more tired than when he went to bed.

Tom had worries about retiring and leaving the boat with his son. He knew that Max (with Nick's help) could run the boat without him, but a nagging part of him didn't want to let go of the business. Once he gave it up, he would never go back on the boat. He would miss the camaraderie, the fights, sarcasm, the cutting jokes and the momentary victory that came with a pot full of crab. He would miss the feeling of being in a fistfight with Mother Nature and coming back for more. No one had ever beaten Mother Nature on her home turf in the Bering Sea. A draw was all he could hope for, but he had come out of the fight still standing thirty-seven years later and that was a source of pride.

Even though he was excited to spend more time with his wife, he had the sinking feeling that the only thing left after he retired was to wait around to die.

"Tom, are you there?" asked Carol, as she tucked her blond hair behind her ear.

Tom looked into his wife's blue eyes for a moment and then noticed a waiter in a white button-up shirt, black tie and long black apron staring at him.

"I think I'm going to need a few more minutes," Tom said, looking up and down the menu for something that he would recognize. "Sorry about that."

The quiet clink of silverware on dishes and the low murmur of conversation made Tom self-conscious of how loudly he was speaking.

"Not a problem, sir." The waiter left.

"Is the boat on your mind?" Carol said, knowing that it was. She knew he was having a tough time with the realization that he was going to have to give it up after the season.

"Yeah, a little." He smiled at her. He knew that she knew better. "But I also don't know what I'm looking at. Why is everything crusted these days? I just want crust-free halibut. Do you think they can do that?"

Carol shrugged. "I'm not sure what the crusting process is."

They smiled at each other.

"What the heck is cerviche?" Tom asked.

"I don't know. But it sounds fancy." Carol shrugged. "I think we should get a bottle of white wine. I'm in the mood."

They had a view of the ocean on a sunny day and nowhere else to be. He would have a glass and a half or so and then walk it off. Carol would get buzzed off of two glasses, and he loved seeing her tipsy and silly.

"Sounds good," Tom said, rubbing his salt-and-pepper beard.

The waiter came and took their orders. Tom was able to get his halibut non-crusted.

They sat and watched the ocean without speaking. The waves rolled in chest-high on the surfers. Tom saw a pair of young lovers walking along the shoreline. For a moment he was jealous, but on further consideration he didn't want to be young again. Most of his youth had been spent on the boat, and he had no desire to start all over.

Tom and Carol had started dating when he was a junior in high school and she was a sophomore, and most of her life had been based around his crabbing schedule. After this season it would be her turn to take the reins of their future. Wherever she wanted to go, within the bounds of their budget, they would go. When they discussed his pending retirement, she smiled and her eyes had a far-off look. Judging from the books lying around the house, he guessed Italy was going to be their first trip.

"It's my last run," he said.

"I know," she said with a smile. "It's your last five-month stretch of work. I can't wait."

"I'm sure you will be sick of me in six months. Just begging me to get back on the boat." He knew it that wasn't true but mild self-deprecation was a part of his personality. When he was on the boat that part of him disappeared.

"Yeah, probably," she said. "But once I blow through our retirement, you'll have to go back to work anyway. I could start working on it now if you want to take me shopping."

Tom responded with a fake glare. Tom hated shopping and she knew it. One of the perks of having a wife was that the only thing he had to shop for was surprises and gifts for her. The mere thought of walking through an overcrowded mall with stores playing loud sounds they called music, while boys who were supposed to be men posed without their shirts or chest hair, made him want to be on the boat. The boat was his place away from everything that he didn't understand.

When they left, Carol made Tom go into only a few stores in the immediate area, and then they called it a day. He loved her for it.

"This is your, uhhhh, captain speaking. The, uhhhh, travel time to Anchorage will be three hours and eleven minutes. Uhhh, the trip looks like it will be smooth sailing but we ask that while you are seated, please keep your seatbelt on in case we hit unexpected turbulence. Thank you."

Nick felt like he was going back to a girlfriend that he couldn't love but never wanted to live without. He looked at the tattoo of a compass on the inside of his right forearm. He told people that he had gotten it so that he would always be able to find his way home, but he really just thought it looked cool. The line about finding his way home was an afterthought that he used to pick up women.

Growing up he had always wanted to leave Alaska in hopes that all of his problems would stay there, but he didn't know anyone anywhere else besides his grandmother in New Mexico and she was losing her marbles. The brutally long and dark winter in Alaska caused him to have mood swings. He didn't know if winter made him bipolar, but it felt like it sometimes.

Flying out of Albuquerque to Seattle felt like a short hop because he was able to drift in and out of sleep for most of the trip, even though he had plastic bags of cash duct-taped to his legs and stomach. Now that he had had some rest, he knew he wouldn't fall asleep between Seattle and Anchorage.

He had half-expected to get arrested during the first few minutes in the airport. In the shuttle bus from Santa Fe down to Albuquerque, he looked behind him to see if there was anyone following him. Every cop he saw was going to be the one who put him away. He had waited for five weeks after the robbery to fly out, hoping that some of the heat from the police had worn off.

When the plane landed under the cover of night in Anchorage, Nick sighed.

The next morning Nick heard a little knock on his bedroom door. The soft taps from low on the door told him it was one of the boys. Nick had been awake about twenty minutes, but hadn't pulled himself out of bed yet. He was thinking about the upcoming crabbing season and dreading the long hours.

"Hello?" said the little voice on the other side of the door.

"Come in," Nick said.

The door opened slowly and Madden looked in.

"Hi Uncle Nick," Madden said with a grin. "We missed you."

"Hey little man," Nick said, scooting over on the bed. "Come on up here. I missed you guys too."

Madden sprinted and tried to leap on the bed. He was only able to get his top half up, so Nick leaned over and pulled him up by his shoulders. Tyler peeked in his head around the door jam but didn't come inside.

"Cool pajamas," Nick said. "Do you want to come in too, Ty?"

Tyler shook his head.

"Thanks. It's Iron Man. Do you know who he is? You don't wear a shirt in bed like Dad."

"I know who Iron Man is and yes, I don't wear a shirt because I get too hot."

"When I get big, I'll probably get too hot too."

Nick propped himself up on the bed with his elbows and Madden did the same. Tyler ran into the room and handed Nick a Hot Wheels car.

"Is this for me?" Nick said. "I love Corvettes."

Tyler nodded. "Thanks. Now I have something to play with on the boat."

Tyler smiled and then ran off, his little footsteps fading down the hallway.

"You guys are leaving to go fishing soon." Madden said it like it was an accusation, or maybe that was just Nick's perception. "Do the crabs pinch you with their claws?" Madden made pinchers with his hands.

Nick said, "Um, sometimes, and it hurts a little but not too much."

"I've been on Grandpa's boat before. He said that it would be mine someday."

"Oh yeah? That's pretty neat."

"Yeah, but I have to share it with Tyler."

"That's fair."

"It's okay I guess. Me and you and Dad and Tyler will all work together on the boat," Madden said.

Nick was stunned. The thought of still working on the boat when Madden was old enough to run it depressed him. He didn't have a retirement plan, or any plan for the future for that matter, so it was clearly possible. Until recently, his only plan had been surviving jail.

"And we'll all look out for each other. That's what brothers do," he said.

"I know," Madden said with the mild condescension that only a six-year-old can generate. "That's what Mom told me. Like you and Dad. You're brothers. Not real brothers but kind of. Mom told me that too."

"Right. We are just like brothers."

"And you'll keep Dad safe when you guys are on the boat? Because Mom gets worried when you guys are gone. I saw her cry once because of it, I think."

"Of course I'll keep your dad safe."

"I told her that Dad is safe when you're around."

"Good. You're a good boy Maddy."

"I know. Time for breakfast. Do you want Fruit Loops?"

"Maybe."

"I'm only allowed to have them once a week because Dad said they make me spaz out so I saved them for today."

"Thanks buddy."

Madden got up and pitter-pattered down the hall. Nick laid back down even though he knew he wouldn't be able to go back to sleep.

1 WEEK BEFORE THE CAPTAIN'S LAST SEASON

When Alexander stepped out of his house it was bright. Not yellow like the sun bright. Pure white. The storm from the night before had left a brilliant, clean slate of snow and there was still a bit falling. The sun reflected off the flakes, casting light where there should have been shadows. Above, the sky was the same white as the snow. It wasn't quite whiteout conditions because he could differentiate between the sky and the ground, but he would have to keep his eye on the weather. Many men older and more experienced than he had found themselves lost on the naked, landmark-free tundra.

Alexander pulled his ski goggles down over his face. He took off a glove and ran his hand around the strap, making sure there weren't any kinks.

He let his dark brown eyes adjust to his now amber-colored world. He had on his lucky winter hat and hoped it would be warm enough. His family only had one helmet and his little sister, Haley, was going to wear it. She wouldn't want to but that was part of their agreement. If she was going to ride with him, she had to wear the helmet. She was the smartest person in their family, and he needed her to protect her brain. Alexander wasn't dumb by any means, but he understood his intellectual limits.

He unhooked the bungee cords holding down the tarp down over the two snowmachines. Then he got up on the trailer, where the snowgos (as the natives say) were sitting, and pulled off the blue tarp. He shook it and the snow slid off the sides. After two tries his lime green Arctic Cat started up. He maintained the snowmachines year-round because his family depended on the food that he brought in from his hunts. Each year he put all of his state-issued dividend check toward the needs of the machines. He didn't want to imagine what they would do if even one of them broke down, because hunting in Alaska is a two-person job.

While they were going out hoping to get some meat, the real reason was that Alexander wanted to spend some time with Haley before he left for crab season.

Alexander backed both machines off the trailer. Haley came out of the house with two backpacks and two guns. The heavier thirty-ought six was for Alexander to carry in case they saw a caribou. Haley slung the twenty-two across her back for rabbit and ptarmigan. Haley smiled when she stood next to Alexander. She had recently become as tall as he was.

"Ready?" Alex said to Haley, who nodded and put on the helmet. Her long black hair spilled out of the bottom and past her shoulders.

Haley climbed onto her machine. She revved her engine a few times and Alexander did the same. They didn't need to rev them but they liked to hear the whirr of the machines.

Alexander eased his machine perpendicular to the road, looked both ways, and pulled out, with Haley following closely behind.

They passed behind Swanson's, the local grocery store, and headed to the Kuskokwim River. Alexander's friend had told him that he shot a few caribou up the river the day before.

Their family had a lot of fish left from the summer season, but Alexander wanted to eat red meat and he couldn't bring himself to buy it at the store. Village beef was overpriced and he questioned how good it was. The meat had to fly up from the Lower 48, through Anchorage and then out to Bethel.

They travelled up the river a few miles on the road that had been plowed to bring groceries and supplies to the villages that surrounded Bethel.

After riding on the road for a short time, they left and created their own trail because the trucks had packed the snow on the road until it turned into ice in various patches.

Cruising up the river, they weaved around each other and played like a pair of lions jogging in the Serengeti. Alexander had the bigger, stronger machine and he sped past Haley on the straightaways, but hers was lighter and more nimble so she could carve her way through the snow, spewing up a brilliant white rooster-tail when she gunned the throttle.

After riding for an hour and a half up the river, they pulled off onto a smaller trail that was fit only for snowmachines. Haley signaled with her left hand like she was eating an invisible sandwich.

They came to a stop and turned off their snowgos.

"You're hungry already?" Alexander said with a sneer. "I thought you were getting in shape because of volleyball. Why do you eat all the time, Piggly Wiggly?"

Haley pulled off her helmet and shook out her hair. "Oh please," she said. "Look at these guns." She put both of her fists up and flexed her biceps.

"I can't even tell if you're flexing or not," Alexander chuckled.

"It's because of my snowsuit, jerk," Haley said with a smile.

Alex turned around and dug through his backpack for their lunches. He found the bologna and processed cheese sandwiches and tossed her one, then pulled out the chips and sodas. The chips had multiplied in number but were exponentially smaller in size due to the jostling of the ride.

They ate in the comfortable silence of siblings.

Alexander finished his sandwich and drained the rest of his soda with a gulp. He tossed the can into the snow against the bottom of the ridge they had parked beside.

He pulled the box of .22 rounds out of his backpack and took off his gloves. Haley finished her sandwich and stuffed the bag into her pocket. Then she threw her can, which landed a little short of Alexander's and to the left. He smiled when he noticed that he got more distance in his throw.

"I guess you need to work out a little more," Alexander said. She pretended not to hear him.

Alexander took out three ten-round clips and loaded them. He pushed the rounds as far back into the clip as possible to reduce the odds of the gun jamming. When the clip was full, he knocked its backside with his hand like a smoker on a new pack of cigarettes.

Haley brought the .22 over from her machine and sat next to Alexander. She handed him the gun. He checked to see if it was loaded and made sure the safety was on. Then he popped in the first clip and slid the bolt backward, putting a bullet in the chamber. He handed the gun back to his sister.

"Safety's on," Alexander said even though she knew he wouldn't hand her a live weapon.

Haley put the stock in her left hand and pulled the gun butt into her right shoulder.

She focused on the soda can and flipped the safety off. She took a deep breath, let out half of it to steady her hands just like she had been taught, and squeezed out bursts of three rounds until only one bullet was left. The can was cut through its center, leaning toward them as if genuflecting.

"On the top of the can," Haley said, calling her shot.

"Through the mouth hole," Alexander challenged her.

"K."

The gun popped.

Haley handed the gun to Alexander, who checked to make sure it wasn't loaded while she trudged through the snow to look at her can.

"Almost perfect," she said, holding up the can. "I barely clipped the side of the mouth hole."

After his turn shooting at the cans, Alexander decided that once they blew through their remaining clip, they would call it a day. He didn't like going home empty-handed but he also didn't feel like chasing the ghosts of some caribou that might not exist.

5 DAYS BEFORE THE CAPTAIN'S LAST SEASON

Even though he didn't want to be a pain, Nick had to ask to borrow Max's car to run some errands. Max wanted to ask Nick what he was up to, but he didn't want Nick to think that he didn't trust him. Their relationship was different now that they had been apart for three and a half years. Max had hoped that Nick would come out of jail and everything would be the way it was before, but it there was a chasm between them. When Nick left the house, Max wanted to say something to him, to tell him that he was glad that Nick was back in their lives and that for the first time in a long time, they could all look toward the future as a family. Instead, Max handed him the keys and told him to drive safe.

Nick sat in Max's SUV and watched the house from up the street. No one appeared to be moving inside. A light snow was falling. Nick had turned off the windshield wipers so that he wouldn't draw attention to himself, but the ambient heat betrayed the car's warmth by melting the snow that landed on the car. Drops of water ran down the windshield, blurring Nick's view.

Nick had gone over the bills he'd taken from the bank and was relieved to see that they weren't sequential. He didn't know if they were marked so he had washed them in the sink at his grandmother's. It felt a little silly, but he hoped it would remove his fingerprints.

He exchanged the money, little by little, through New Mexico's many casinos. Soon he had a completely different stack of bills than the one he had taken from the bank. As Nick suspected, even though he never saw them, the police had been watching the casinos that were close to Santa Fe. He slid under their radar with his $10 and $20 bets. He lost a little on some days, won a little on others. All in all, he was around $600 short of what he had started with.

After the washing, he only handled the money while wearing latex gloves in his grandmother's house. When he exchanged small amounts of the cash for casino chips, he put a small dab of superglue on his fingertips so he wouldn't leave a print. One of the cons in his cellblock had taught him that.

After a few minutes, having not seen anyone, Nick got out of the car, jogged over to the mailbox that said Williams on the side, and put the envelope full of cash in it. He knew the money wouldn't cover all of the hospital bills, but it would help.

3 DAYS BEFORE THE CAPTAIN'S LAST SEASON

Max was cooking steaks, and hot dogs for the kids, on the grill. He was relieved that Nick hadn't taken him up on the offer to stay for the last meal with his family before flying out to Dutch Harbor.

People in the Lower 48 would have thought he was crazy for standing outside and grilling when it was only a few degrees above freezing, but the cold air was invigorating. He looked out beyond his yard into the Cook Inlet, named after Captain Cook who led an expedition there in 1778. He wondered what it had been like more than 200 years ago on the open ocean. It was bad enough in the high-end cold weather raingear that he had packed into his waterproof duffle bag. He still got cold and he had the best that modern technology offered. To be out on the water with only wool to protect him from the cold would've been torture.

Julie opened the back door, snapping Max out of his daydream. "How long until the steaks are done?"

"Not much longer," Max said. "I'm making sure that yours is basically a hockey puck."

"Rare is so gross," she smiled. Max had teased her about that since their second date. He was too nervous on their first date to tease her about anything. "I'll start rounding up the kids."

"Thanks." He stood outside for a few more minutes and wondered why he worked a job that took him away from his family and made him ineligible for life insurance. The stomping of little feet and shuffling chairs brought him out of his thoughts. He knew he would miss even the small things like the sounds of his family.

After dinner he went up to the boys' room to tuck them in. When they woke in the morning he would be gone.

"All right boys. Sleep tight, okay?" Max liked that his boys had chosen to stay in the same room. They were only six and four and he figured there would be plenty of time for them to not get along once they were teenagers.

Max sat on Madden's bed while Tyler snored softly. "You're the man of the house while I'm gone, okay?" Max whispered to keep from waking up Tyler.

"Dad, I don't want you to leave," Madden said with a quiver in his voice.

Max knew he was ten seconds away from making his son cry.

"I know. I don't want to leave either. Some day you will be proud of me and what I'm doing."

"I would be proud if you stayed, Dad. I promise I would be."

Max exhaled, kissed his son on his forehead and left the room before he decided to quit his job. He didn't know that Julie had been standing in the hallway and had heard the whole exchange.

After Max dropped him off at his hotel for the night, Nick went to the liquor store across the street. It was the same dirty store that was across the street from every dingy hotel in the country. He bought a bottle of tequila and a six-pack of Bud Light. He had told himself that he was going to have a few beers and a couple of pulls off the bottle and call it a night, but after watching some TV he was restless.

Nick called a cab and took it to the only strip bar in Anchorage, Cheeks.

The first time Nick went to a strip club and hung out with one of the girls, he relaxed and enjoyed the pseudo-intimacy. He liked strippers because they didn't want anything. They wouldn't ever want to meet his family or his friends. Unlike most of the men in the bar, Nick didn't have delusions about taking any of the women home with him.

He walked past the short line of guys standing outside, gave one of the bouncers a nod, and shook the other's hand. Inside the colored lights and loud music hit him all at once, but the thing that affected him the most was the smell. It was a mix of testosterone and body spray that was somewhere in between bad and good, depending on the concentrations of each.

A stage dominated the middle of the huge room. Around it were velvet-covered benches with low, cubicle-style walls that customers could see over so that if they wanted a lap dance, they could have a little privacy. Across from the stage, a bar ran along the length of the wall.

Above the floor, a random assortment of moving lights and disco balls spun colors around the room.

Nick sat alone on the lowest tier of benches. For a weeknight, the place was pretty full. The club was a mix of single creepy older guys and groups of younger guys celebrating. In every batch of younger guys, there was always one who had been over-served and was struggling to stand up.

After watching the woman pander to the guys on the rail surrounding the stage for a few verses of a Motley Crue song, Nick looked around for someone to buy a beer from. A brunette in a bikini approached him.

"Hey sweetie, are you looking for a drink?" She batted her fake eyelashes in a way that made her seem like a character in a movie instead of a real person.

"Um, yeah," Nick replied. He thought that he should have said something more clever but that was all he could muster.

"I'll buy you a beer if you buy a dance from me."

Nick had planned on getting a dance or four at some time during the night so he figured it was an even trade.

"Deal," he said.

She left and came back with a beer a moment later.

"Jesus," he said. "Was that beer in your purse?"

"No," she replied with a giggle. "The bartenders serve me fast because I'm special."

"I guess so. Have a seat." Nick scooted over to give her room. "What's your name?"

"Jennifer."

"Your name is Jennifer? Shouldn't it be Dolce or Cinnamon?"

"Yeah, but I wanted something simple."

"All right then."

"What's your name?"

"My name is Jennifer as well." Nick thought that if she got to lie, then he would lie as well.

"Oh really? What are the odds?" She was smiling.

"My mom wanted to name me Jasmine or Bubbles but they settled on Jenny because it was simple," he said, more to amuse himself than her.

Jennifer laughed and put her hand on his arm. "Do you want me to dance to the next song?"

Her simple contact made him spellbound. "Sure."

Over the speaker system the DJ said, "Give it up for Heaven. Heaven everybody." Nick assumed that the DJ was referring to the stripper on stage and not the celestial destination for sinless Christians, but either way, both were worth clapping for.

A smattering of disinterested applause came from the crowd. Then a song by Jay-Z came on.

The music thumped. "Jennifer" walked away from Nick and then slowly made her way toward him.

Thump, thump, thump, went the music. She stood between his legs by his knees and bounced.

Nick never knew where he was supposed to look. Jennifer was maintaining eye contact with him but he thought it would be dismissive not to check out her body. She was the one in a bikini and had clearly avoided food for a long time. He didn't want to be disrespectful or just another creepy guy, but he also thought that the fact that he had been there so many times before he went to jail clearly established his creepy status.

When he looked at her eyes, he knew that she wasn't interested in anything more than his money, despite her playful manner. Her black-lined eyes roamed the bar, searching for her next customer. As he followed her sightline, he realized that he couldn't stare at anything for more than five seconds or whatever he saw - the girls, the stage lights, the booths - went from visually stimulating to depressing.

After the song finished, he was disgusted with himself. Jennifer asked him if he wanted another dance but he declined. He got up and went back to the hotel feeling lonelier than ever.

Alexander's blue and gold Bethel Regional High Warriors duffle bag was packed so full that he thought the seams were going to come apart. He worried that the zipper would break from all the jostling in the plane's cargo area, so he put a few safety pins in his pocket just in case.

Leaving his sister behind was never easy, but the money he would make, combined with the yearly check from the state for oil revenue and subsistence hunting, would keep them in the black for most of the year, barring unforeseen incidents.

Their mother was rarely around and even though they lived in a town of less than seven thousand people, they had only spoken to their father a handful of times. When he left his sister, Alexander was leaving her without any family to rely on.

As his plane took off, he looked out at the series of interconnected lakes and rivers that made up the area surrounding his hometown and sighed.

2 DAYS BEFORE THE CAPTAIN'S LAST SEASON

Tom watched the harbor crew lower his boat into the water after it had been dry-docked for part of the summer. There were a few seams that had to be fixed on the bow. Nothing serious, but he had enough worries without having to think about holes in his boat.

He went on board and walked around. It was a little dusty but nothing that the guys couldn't take care of before they shipped off. He used to pay some of the local women in Dutch Harbor to clean the boat, but times were lean. He would still pay the same ladies to clean up after their trip. Having six guys in a confined area without a washer and dryer for two to three weeks at a time could turn the cleanest place funky.

Most days, Tom was able to keep the accident with Chuck out of his head, but every time he got back on the boat at the beginning of the season it came roaring back. After losing Chuck, more than fifteen seasons ago, everything about crabbing had changed for him, but nothing on the boat was different. It was the same boat, with most of the same equipment. Even though he had heard stories his whole life from his father and other crabbers about the dangers of the Bering Sea, its constant shifts and how the wind and the waves could go in different directions, he had always felt like everything happened to other people. Bad things didn't happen to him or his crew. After Chuck, he worried about his crew so much during the season that he developed a peptic ulcer from taking too much ibuprofen for his stress headaches. He told himself that he would tell his wife about it after the season if the symptoms persisted. It wasn't a big deal. The symptoms of his ulcer only showed up while he was on the boat.

The worst part about the accident with Chuck was that it could have been avoided. It wasn't a rogue wave that no one saw coming, or one of the other hundreds of ways that the sea can take a man. It was the simple coiling rope that connected the pot to the two buoys that would be used to raise it later.

When the seven-hundred-pound pot went over the side of the boat and rapidly made its descent to the ocean floor, the cord wrapped around Chuck's leg and brought him down with it.

The men screamed at Tom to stop the boat. They yelled "man overboard" so loudly that he could still hear their cries.

Tom backed the boat up and the men hooked the line to cut it at the buoys in hope that it would relieve the tension and Chuck would be able to set himself free.

They didn't find Chuck for another forty-five minutes. Even if Chuck had been able to get himself free of the rope, the water was too cold to survive in for more than five minutes.

When the crew spotted the body, Tom and Jack went out in a dingy to retrieve it. As the captain, Tom knew that it was his job to take care of the body. Jack had volunteered to go with him and for that Tom was eternally thankful. He didn't blame any of the men for not wanting to pull their friend out of the water.

Jack, a red-haired fellow who was built like a refrigerator, rowed the dingy over to the body, which was floating face down. Chuck's orange rain suit with the boat's name in black marker on the back stood out against the gray skies and dark blue water.

Tom reached down and tried to get a grip on the body. He grabbed Chuck by his arms. Chuck was an average-size guy so Tom thought he could pull him onto the boat by himself, but the position was awkward and Tom didn't have the strength without the water's buoyancy supporting Chuck's weight. Jack had to come over and help.

One good pull by both men and Chuck was in the boat. For a moment Tom saw a resemblance between Chuck and Nick and it took his breath away. They had the same dark brown hair and lean build. Tom closed his eyes. It took focus for him to shake the image from his head.

Water drained from Chuck's rain suit into the dingy. His face was pale blue and his eyes were still open. Tom thought it was strange that Chuck didn't have a terrified look on his face. Instead he appeared relaxed.

They returned to the ship and the men hauled up the dingy with the hydraulic lift. The men didn't leave the area, but they didn't get close to the body either. It was as if the body had a twenty-foot impenetrable force field around it that none of the men dared to test.

Tom had Jack turn the ship around so that they could head back to Dutch Bay. He got a blanket to put over Chuck. He wanted to respect his privacy. Tom knew he wouldn't want to be seen like that. Chuck was a good man, and he had worked hard for Tom for the last six years. He never complained or get into scraps with the other crew members. Now it was all over.

On the way back to port, Tom knew that their season was all but finished and the men wouldn't make very much money. There was only two days left in the season and by the time they took the body back the season would be over. He also knew that they wouldn't even think about the money they'd missed out on until much later. All they would think about was how it could've been them.

PART 2

15 DAYS LEFT IN RED KING CRAB SEASON

National Weather Service Advisory: SW WIND 40 KT. SEAS 12 FT. PATCHY FOG. RAIN.

The pots were loaded and the six men were on board. The only new element was the greenhorn that Tom had hired. He found it difficult to keep the same crew. Along with Nick's spot, which had been vacant for three seasons, there was a second open slot most years due to competition with other boats and people moving on to more stable work.

There were crewmembers who had thought they were tough until they spent time on the Bering Sea. Men who were much stronger in the weight room than anyone on the boat would wear out after a few days and quit. A man had to have endurance, not brute strength, to work for twenty hours in a row. Throw in seasickness and sleep deprivation, and men would crumble from exhaustion.

Tom met the greenhorn on the dock and brought him on board to introduce him to the crew. During the introductions Max cut the new guy off and told him that they were going to call him greenhorn until he earned a name.

The greenhorn said hi to Mike, the gray-bearded engineer, as he walked by. Mike responded, "Yeah, yeah."

"That's Mike," Max said. "Don't worry about him. He doesn't like anyone, including himself."

"Fuck you Max," Mike said without turning around.

"See?" Max said to the greenhorn.

The greenhorn thought he was going to like Max. They continued their short tour of the boat.

"Hey sweet tits," Nick said from the other side of the boat, pulling back his welder's mask. He was fixing a crack on the rail. Nick stood up. "Hey, I'm Nick," he said, offering his hand as he began to approach them.

When the greenhorn reached to shake, Nick pulled his hand back and said, "Psych, not yet. Handshakes have to be earned."

Max laughed.

"Hey, Green, I hope I shake your hand after the season, all right?" Nick said, pulling his skull-painted welder's helmet over his face.

"All right," the greenhorn responded. He felt better knowing that acceptance could be earned.

Tom went downstairs to the engine room. Before going inside he put on earmuffs and prepared himself for the engine's dull roar.

He saw Mike bent over, facing away from him. He took a wrench from the desk and slid it on the ground into Mike's foot. Mike turned.

"Hey," Tom yelled. "How are things?"

"Okay," Mike yelled back, making the okay sign with his hand.

"How many more years do we got left?"

"Fifteen. Twenty at most."

His answer startled Tom. "Not us. I meant the boat."

Mike sneered. "Not that long, that's for damn sure."

"Will it hold up for the season?"

"I have no reason to think otherwise."

Tom nodded and turned to leave. He would've preferred a simple yes.

Max and Nick finished their prep work on the boat and decided to have a few drinks at the Brass Buckle.

Out of habit, the boys asked for Tom's permission to leave the boat. Tom only asked that they didn't go looking for trouble. Nick responded that he never had to look – trouble always knew where he was. Tom and Max laughed, but Nick wasn't trying to be funny.

It was an unspoken agreement that they would only have a few drinks before calling it a night. Neither wanted to start the season with a hangover. They had done that plenty of times in their early twenties with poor results.

The guys who didn't get crab work but lived in the small town of Unalaska resented the guys who did have work, and insults would fly. Or guys who liked to get drunk and fight would have seven or eight drinks and then want to complete their night.

Inside the bar, Nick looked around. Two guys were passed out with their heads on the table, and several other guys were scattered around the bar. All of them were alone. The only sound in the bar was a show on the television about Alaska state troopers.

No matter how hard he tried not to, Nick always looked at the wall lined with pictures of lost fisherman and the Coast Guard press releases underneath them. Every time he walked by his eyes stopped on Chuck's picture. He only knew about Chuck through Tom as a cautionary tale about how dangerous the boat can be. He didn't know many of the men, there were accidents every year, but even a few felt like too many.

The bar was against the back wall with a dozen stools in front of it. The wine glass rack hanging over the bar was empty.

Behind the bar stood a slender woman in her late 50s with dyed black hair, a red Salty Dog Saloon hooded sweatshirt and faded jeans. Nick thought that she must have been pretty before the smoke in the bar and the stress of dealing with drunken assholes took its toll on her face. When she noticed the guys, she came out from behind the bar.

"Hey Rhonda," Nick said.

"Holy shit, sugar, you're out," Rhonda said, giving Nick a hug. "You boys leave tomorrow right? I thought I saw Ms. Remorse at the dock."

"Yes ma'am," Max said.

"Don't ma'am me, damn it," Rhonda said to Max, putting her hands on their backs and leading them to the bar. "I feel old enough as it is. It's like I'm in purgatory with these bunch of bums."

They settled into their bar stools while Rhonda went around the bar.

"What are you boys having?"

"Double Jack, up," Nick said, giving two quick thumbs up. His response was quick enough to earn a look from Rhonda and Max.

"Is that how tonight is going to go?" Max said.

"If we're only going to have a couple of drinks then I want to make them count," Nick said. "Now that you're old and married I'm sure that Rhonda can conjure up an O'Doul's for you."

"We don't carry that garbage here and you know it," Rhonda responded with a smile.

"Make it two," Max said, turning to Nick. "We're the same age and you know it."

"I don't know about that. Having kids makes you old."

"So does three years in the pen."

"Fuck," Nick paused and let it sink in. "You aren't kidding."

Rhonda got out the bottle of Jack Daniels and poured each of them three fingers. As she passed them the glasses, the bar door opened and her eyes widened.

Max and Nick turned and saw three guys too clean-cut to be locals and too clean-shaven to be fisherman. They were Coasties.

Fishermen and the Coast Guard have had an uneasy alliance as long as both have existed. A boat might get busted for illegal fishing activities, or the crew might need to be saved by the Coasties if their ship is sinking. Either way, when the Coast Guard was headed toward a fishing boat, bad things were probably happening.

The first Coastie chose a seat two stools down from Nick. The other two sat on the far side.

"How are you fellows doing today?" one of the men asked Nick.

Before Nick could respond, one of the previously sleeping men stumbled towards the bar and pointed at the Coasties.

"You assholes took…" the man said, while wiping the drool from his slumber off of his face. His hat was tilted sideways and one of his shoes was untied. He tried to support himself on the corner of a table when it tipped over, he fell with it.

Everyone stayed quiet for a moment to see if the man would continue his tirade. He remained on the floor. The men turned back to the bar.

Rhonda checked the Coasties' IDs. They were old enough to be in the bar, but not by much. They each ordered a light beer.

As Rhonda slid beers to the men, Nick said, "Put those on our tab," without making eye contact.

"You don't have to do that," one of the men said.

"Yes, I do," Nick responded. "That's the way it's been long before you were born. If you ever see me floating around somewhere out there, fish me out, okay?"

"Thank you," the young man responded.

"We appreciate your service," Max said.

Nick nodded, ending the conversation.

After they settled up, Rhonda came around the bar and hugged them both.

"I'll see you boys when you get back, okay?"

"Of course," Max said. "First round is on you?"

She laughed.

"My pleasure. Be safe," she said as she walked away. She stopped and turned around. "No press releases this season. You got that?"

Neither responded, though they both glanced at the wall of pictures.

14 DAYS LEFT IN RED KING CRAB SEASON

National Weather Service Advisory: NE WIND 25 KT. SEAS 11 FT

Tom pulled anchor at 5:00 a.m. sharp. His crew had slept on the boat. When Tom first started crabbing, he and the rest of the crew would stay at a hotel. Some guys would go out drinking and sleep past the time the boats were shipping out, causing boats to leave shorthanded. But now leaving without a full crew wasn't an option. The Alaska Fish and Game Department set quotas and if a boat didn't fulfill its quota, it risked having a smaller one the next year. Smaller quotas meant less money. Once a boat lost a cut of the crab, other boats would work to fill in what was missing.

For the last few years Tom had wondered if he had made the right decision becoming the ship's captain. His older brother, Everett, had taken a desk job with seafood processors. It was a safe 9:00 – 5:00 gig with a pension and benefits. But ultimately, it was boring.

If Tom hadn't taken the helm, his family would have had to sell the boat, and he couldn't stand the thought of letting his father's legacy disappear. All of the close calls in the storms, the stresses of whether they were going to catch crab that year, and losing one of his crew members had worn him down. He had sacrificed a lot keeping the boat above water and full of crab. Now, much closer to the end of his life than the beginning, he had a hard time convincing himself that sacrificing time with his family and putting his life at risk had been worth it.

As they left the harbor, Tom looked at the Russian Orthodox crosses that dotted the hillside. His father used to remind his crew over the intercom as they left port that the sea, like the Lord, giveth and taketh away. Even though he discontinued the practice after his father died, he heard every word in his head as his boat cut through Iliuliuk Bay and into the open ocean.

Nick's alarm clock went off. The greenhorn snored above him. Nick sat up, hunching his back so he wouldn't hit his head, and pulled on his long johns and fleece pants. He put on a long-sleeved teeshirt over the one that he wore in bed and then a hoodie.

"Wakey, wakey, motherfuckers," Nick bellowed at the top of his lungs. Upstairs in his captain's chair, Tom smiled. Tom couldn't hear the words that Nick was saying but he knew the sound of Nick's bellow. Nick always woke like he had been shocked by a car battery, which made him worth his weight in gold on the boat. Tom didn't like having to go downstairs to wake his crew because he would piss them off enough barking orders over the course of the trip.

Another thing about Nick that Tom loved was that he gave the crew heart. Tom didn't care if his men hated each other as long as they were willing and able to fight. Every pound of crab had to be earned. If a man didn't have guts, he shouldn't be on the boat.

Nick slid back the curtains on the other bunks. Two were empty. One was Tom's and the other was Mike's. Mike was a former Marine, and no one wakes up before an old Marine. Besides being the engineer, Mike was the cook, so he was already putting enough bacon, eggs and toast to feed twice the number of men that they had on board.

The first time that Mike heard Nick yelling at the crew to get up, he thought he was going to find him dead in his bunk the next morning. Mike thought that Nick would calm down over time, but that was more than 10 years ago. The season before Nick went to jail, one of his shipmates became so angry at Nick's morning antics that he took a swing at him. All the disgruntled fellow got for his efforts was a busted nose and his walking papers from Tom.

"You lazy old crones wake up. It's the captain's retirement season so let's fill this puppy up," Nick said, increasing his volume while trying not to laugh. "You're on the Ms. Remorse. The Broad of the Bering Sea. The Countess of Crab. Woooowwwweeeee. It's a great day to either catch crab or die, and I'm living, brother, I'm living."

"All right, all right," Max said. "Just shut the fuck up."

"You want Daddy to get in there and hump you awake?" Nick said. He started to paw at Max's hair and face. "You like that, sweetness?"

"You guys should just have sex and get it over with," said the greenhorn from the top bunk.

Alexander rolled over and put his pillow over his head.

"Oooo, I'm trying. Daddy's been in jail and he's lonely," Nick said, happy that the greenhorn was up. "You're next, newbie. Fresh meat."

Max swung his fist backward at Nick but got nothing but air. Nick grabbed Max's pillow out from under his head and threw it across the room to his own bunk.

"Let's have some fun," Nick said, walking to the kitchen.

"Where are you from?" Alexander asked the greenhorn as they sat at the dining table eating their first meal on board.

"Wasilla," the greenhorn replied sheepishly.

"Well, fuck," Nick said. "Sarah Palin country. What the hell's in the water out there? Lead? Mercury?"

"Good Lord almighty," Max bellowed. "Did you have a part in unleashing that moron on America? She's embarrassed the whole damn state and it's a huge state."

"She isn't that bad," said the greenhorn, shifting in his seat.

Alexander leaned forward and let his forehead thump on the table in disgust.

"I wouldn't have voted for that genius if you paid me," Nick said.

"You can't vote," Max said.

"Fair point," Nick said.

Max leaned back, pulled the CB from the wall behind him, and chirped the mike. "Hey Captain." He was taught to call his father captain while they were on the ship to avoid favoritism – even though his shipmates knew he was the captain's son – and to show him the same respect that everyone else on the boat showed. "We have a Palin fan on board."

"No politics on board. That's how people end up in the ocean," Tom said. The sound of wind blowing on the crow's nest could be heard over the mike. "Young, Stevens, even Frank's kid, those are real politicians. Not Palin. Instead of sitting on your thumbs why doesn't one of you teach Sarah Palin how to make bait?"

The guys in the kitchen heard the captain shift in his seat.

"Sarah goddamn Palin." Then the mike went dead.

Max stood up from the table. "Come on Sarah," he said. He headed to the gear room without waiting.

13 DAYS LEFT IN RED KING CRAB SEASON

National Weather Service Advisory: NE WIND 13 KT. SEAS 8 FT

When Nick got outside on deck, he pulled Sarah from the fish grinder that sat in the middle of the boat. On the other side of the boat was the hydraulic lift and the square crab pot mount. No matter how hard the wind blew, the area surrounding the grinder smelled like a dumpster at a seafood restaurant.

Nick went to the front of the boat, and Sarah followed.

"All right," Nick said, handing Sarah a life vest while putting his on. "We need to go to the top of the stack and start untying the pots so that we can bait and then sink them."

Nick grabbed one of the ties, and untied it slowly. "Did you catch that?"

"Yeah," the greenhorn responded.

"Are you sure? Because once we are twenty feet up on a rocking boat with the wind and rain blowing in our grills, I'm not going to want to show you again."

"How about one more time? Just in case."

"Good idea." Nick smiled and showed him again.

Then he climbed up on the pot stack with Sarah following.

"Stay low," Nick said. "You don't want the wind to push you around."

The boat hit a wave and the men rocked back and forth on the stack.

"Whoa," the greenhorn said.

"Yeah," Nick said with a smile. "Whoa is right. You look a little green in the gills."

Sarah kept his head down and started to work on his ties. Nick stood up and spread his arms.

"Owwwwww," Nick howled.

"Okay, okay," Tom said over the intercom as he felt his stomach turn. "Finish the job. I want you guys off the stack ASAP."

When they finished untying the pots, Nick signaled Max who was working the lift. Max directed the hook on top of the lift over to Nick, who connected it to the pot with rope.

Once the pot was on deck, Alexander opened the pot, attached the bait inside and closed it.

With a different set of controls, Max dumped the pot into the water. Alexander threw the buoys overboard.

Nick climbed down from the pots, grinning, while the greenhorn swallowed hard and focused on trying not to throw up.

10 DAYS LEFT IN RED KING CRAB SEASON

National Weather Service Advisory: NW WIND 10KT
BECOMING 20 KT IN THE AFTERNOON. SEAS 7 FT.

"Shit," Nick said.

They were halfway through the first string of pots and they still hadn't caught a crab. Sandfleas were eating the bait before the crabs had a chance to get it.

The men were agitated and approaching rage. Every word spoken had an air of aggression to it. The volatility on the boat reminded Nick of basketball games in the prison yard after a lunchtime scuffle. It didn't help that the men were dealing with their first bout of sleep deprivation from working twenty-hour days.

Alexander didn't smoke, but when Max offered him a cigarette, he couldn't resist. It was a break in the monotony. Max knew it was a bad habit (he only smoked on the boat, away from Julie), but it also gave him a warm sensation, like he was wearing a velvet blanket.

Nick came over to Max and reached into his friend's pocket for sunflower seeds. As the hydraulic lift operator, Max was the only one on deck partially protected from the elements because the controls were placed under an overhang to keep them dry.

Nick packed a bunch of seeds into his cheek. With his couple days of scruff and winter hat he could have passed for a chewing tobacco spokesman.

As the boat approached the next pot, Nick came out from under the deck and grabbed the grappling hook.

Two buoys were connected by a rope, which ran down to the pot resting on the seafloor. Nick's job was to throw the hook into the six-foot span between the buoys and pull the line back to the ship. Once he had the line, he would attach it to the lift and pull up the pot.

Anyone could make a majority of the throws in calm seas, but a good thrower had to make them with the boat, the wind and the rough water all going in different directions. With only seven-foot waves, the weather was as nice as it gets on the Bering Sea, and Nick was able to make the toss with ease. His trick was throwing to where he thought the buoys were going to be, not to where they were. Even though he had failed math class, he was almost perfect in calculating the changing variables.

As Nick pulled the buoys on board and wrapped the line around the lift, he thought about the girl he killed. He had been able to push her out of his mind while on the boat because if he wasn't focused, he could get injured. Now that he was exhausted his mind wandered.

"Nick," Max yelled. "Move."

Nick stepped away from the coiler and signaled for Max to haul the pot up. The lift whirred and produced another empty pot, dripping and with a piece of seaweed hanging from the bottom. The pot was dangling over the deck when the boat took an unexpected roll, causing the 700-pound pot to swing towards Nick.

Nick saw a flash in the corner of his eye. Thanks to years of fighting, he ducked instead of looking, saving himself from serious trauma if not worse. The pot grazed the hood of Nick's raincoat as it swung past him. He scrambled to get out of the way in case it fell on its way back.

"Control that fucking pot," yelled the captain over the intercom.

Max flipped the switches on his control pad while the men on deck ran from the pot. He set it down safely. The men tied it down with the other pots, where they would stay until the boat traveled to more fertile grounds.

Max looked over at Nick, expecting a profanity-ridden tirade.

Nick smiled politely while giving him the finger. Max shrugged and shook his head. Nick walked over to Max and reached into his other pocket. He pulled out a smoke and put it in his mouth. After watching Nick struggle to light the cigarette with his shaky hands, Max took the lighter and sparked it for him. The boat continued on to the next pot.

9 DAYS LEFT IN RED KING CRAB SEASON

National Weather Service Advisory: S WIND 20 BECOMING E 40 KT IN THE AFTERNOON. SEAS 14 FT.

Within the boat's 112 feet, from bow to stern, there were six masculine men. With little or no crab coming in, small slights turned into big ones.

An empty pot gives no hint that there is anything at the bottom of the ocean. A pot with all female or undersized crabs would have at least shown that there were crabs in the area. All of that hard work for nothing.

The weather didn't help the crew's attitude. The wind ripped from bow to stern and the waves caused the men to stagger rather than walk. The captain didn't mind the jokes about mutiny and grumbles that he was losing his touch in his old age because it helped to blow off steam. He would rather have them use him as the common enemy than turn on Sarah or each other because on deck it was dangerous. Besides, he had his father's crowbar under his desk just in case things got hairy. It was put there originally as a joke and over the years had never been pulled out. He didn't plan on pulling it, but there was some comfort in knowing that it was there.

When Max swung a pot by Nick's head for the second time, Tom didn't intervene, even though he didn't like what was going to happen. The ship was getting a little too intense for his comfort.

Once the pot was under control and on deck, Max lit a cigarette and walked out and stood in front of Nick. Then he put his hands behind his back and closed his eyes. The rest of the crew stopped what they were doing to watch.

Tom sighed as he watched from his captain's chair. He wished that he had never started the ridiculous tradition.

Per the rules, Nick began to count to ten. If the count got to ten, his chance for retribution would have passed. Alexander turned away.

"One, two, three, four, five, six, seven…" then Nick punched Max in the stomach.

Sarah lurched forward to intervene, but Alexander grabbed his arm and shook his head.

Max spit out his cigarette and doubled over, almost going to the ground before Nick grabbed his shoulders. Nick pulled Max up, gave him a quick hug and patted him on the back.

"Idiots," Tom mumbled, and resumed looking over his navigational charts.

"You okay?" Nick asked.

"Yeah," Max gasped. "Good one. But I think you pulled it a little."

"Maybe, but I won't next time."

"Fair enough," Max said on the way back to his post.

8 DAYS LEFT IN RED KING CRAB SEASON

National Weather Service Advisory: W WIND 5 KT. LIGHT SNOW.

It was 7:00 a.m., almost time to wake the boys up, and a few more hours until the sun made its short appearance. Snow fell on his windshield and the wipers rhythmically brushed it away.

Tom had finished talking to Carol and was about to hang up when she said, "Remind Nick to call in to his probation officer. He couldn't get in touch with him and Nick didn't tell him he was going to be on the boat. His lawyer was looking for him and asked that I pass along the message."

"He's a big boy," Tom said. "He knows what he's supposed to do. Love you."

"Okay, thanks for reminding him," Carol responded. "I love you too."

Then she hung up before Tom responded. Tom found her guerrilla phone tactics annoying and funny at the same time. She knew that he would remember to tell Nick.

Tom smoked a cigarette and drank the sludge he called coffee, thick enough that a spoon could stand straight up in it.

"Blaaaaa," was the sound coming out of Sarah. Nick and Max stood ten feet behind him, far enough so that if the wind changed direction, they would stay out of the spray.

"Hey Sarah, are you going to be okay?" Max asked. "Thanks for chumming the waters."

The greenhorn pulled his head back from over the side of the boat. "Ulp, I think...blaaaa."

"You almost had it," Nick said. "Be sure to get plenty of fluids."

"Yeah, and don't think about swallowing raw eggs," Max said with a smile. "That won't help."

Nick looked at Max, startled. "You stole my line."

"Your line? I made up that line."

"My ass you did," Nick said, giving Max a friendly shove. They started wrestling on the deck while the seagulls squawked in disapproval.

Tom's tinny voice came on over the intercom. "Knock it off. You guys know that grab-ass on deck leads to injuries. You look like two ducks humping a marmot."

"What does that even mean?" Nick said, letting Max out of a headlock.

"I think it's an insult," Max said.

"To us or the marmot?"

"Shit. I don't know. Maybe the ducks," Max said. He looked over to the still-puking greenhorn. "Hey Sarah, think about two ducks fucking a marmot. That might help."

"Nick, call your probation officer," Tom said over the intercom.

"What's that about?" Max said.

"I'm supposed to check in with him but I don't want to even think about jail or anything to do with it," Nick said. "I love being on the boat and I'm trying to put all of that behind me."

"Isn't calling to check in better than going to jail?"

"I don't want to think about jail or Kelly right now. Let just catch some crab, okay?" Nick walked away without waiting for an answer.

Sarah looked back at them, shook his head and continued throwing up.

7 DAYS LEFT IN RED KING CRAB SEASON

National Weather Service Advisory: VARIABLE WIND 15 KT
WITH GUSTS TO 30 KT. SEAS 9 FT.

"Cock-a-doodle doooo you sons of bitches," Nick yelled.
"Today's the day we catch crabs!"

"Seriously Nick, what's wrong with you?" grumbled Max.

"Not being cooped up in a cage with guys who want to either
stab me or hump me makes me happy," Nick responded.

"I'll do both if you just shut up," said Sarah from above
Nick's bunk.

"You'll have to buy me dinner first!" Nick said, running his
hands roughly over Sarah's face.

Sarah fought him off. Nick started to go to the kitchen when
he turned around and went back to his bunk. He fished around
in his bag, found the Corvette Tyler had given him and put it in
his pocket. He didn't know if it was lucky, but he hoped so.

"I told you bastards that today was going to be the day we caught crab," Nick said with a triumphant smile amid the hoots and hollers of the crew.

No one bothered to remind him that he said that every morning.

The pot was hoisted over the sorting table and Max bounced it up and down to shake the crabs out.

"Hey Nick," said Sarah as they sorted the crabs that had just come in. All the female and undersized crabs went back into the ocean. The males that were large enough were put into a wheelbarrow and dumped into a hole in the deck that went to the live well underneath the boat. "Where did the name of the boat come from?"

"Ms. Remorse? It was the name of Max's grandfather's boat, the one they had before they bought this one, but the captain kept the name. His grandparents got a divorce and Max's grandma, who came from a lot of money, was able to convince the court to give her everything but the boat. It was originally called Ms. Opportunity because of the way his grandparents met." Nick tossed a flounder that had swam into the pot over the rail of the boat. "They were passing each other on the street and his grandfather, Tom Sr., said to her that if he didn't introduce himself, then he would wonder for the rest of his life about the missed opportunity. After the divorce, Tom Sr. wanted to change the name to the Ms. Bitch Who Took Everything But This Goddamn Boat, but the Coasties wouldn't let him register it under that name so he went with Ms. Remorse."

"Women," Sarah said, shaking his head.

"It's not them, it's us," Nick replied. "Now pay attention to what you're doing."

4 DAYS LEFT IN RED KING CRAB SEASON

National Weather Service Advisory: SE WIND 10 KT. FOG.

Tom loved the feel of fog on the ocean. On the open water, the view was seemingly without end, but fog provided a finiteness to the surroundings that gave Tom a sense of comfort.

Tom picked up the phone. "Ms. Remorse."

He wasn't used to getting unexpected calls. Most of the communication was done over CB skipper to skipper, unless it was an emergency. He was focused on keeping the crab coming in and his men safe. He didn't have time to chat someone up.

There was a pause. He could hear someone on the other side of the phone.

"Hello?" Tom said.

"Hi," said the trembling female voice. "Can I speak to my brother Alexander?"

"Is this an emergency or can he call you back?' Tom said more shortly than he intended. He was struggling to see the buoys through the fog.

"Um, our father died."

"Oh," Tom said. "Hold on a few minutes."

Tom pushed the hold button and sighed. He wasn't good at handling other people's emotional crises. When he tried to comfort someone everything that came out of his mouth was a cliché.

"Alexander, please come up here real quick." Tom said over the intercom. Immediately he regretted saying "real quick." Tom wasn't aware of Alexander's relationship with his father, but knew that no one wants to find out his dad died.

Alexander came up. Tom stepped away from his captain's chair and handed him the phone.

"Hello?" Alexander said, surprised at getting a call.

Tom watched Alexander until he realized that he was imposing on a private moment, then he turned to watch the men on deck.

Alexander hung up the phone.

"We can finish this string and take you back to Dutch," Tom said. "That will give us a chance to skip out on the storm coming our way as well."

"No," Alexander said. "We need to catch our fill. We can all use the money. We need to start the season by getting ahead in case we don't do as well catching the other crabs."

"I'll still give you a share of our haul. You don't need to worry about that."

"But I don't want to be given a share. I want to earn it. Besides, I didn't even know my father. I know you better than I know him."

"Look Alexander, you've been great to us and I think you'll regret..."

"I'll regret it more if I leave. Can I please stay and keep working?"

"Sure."

Alexander left the wheelhouse before Tom could say anything else.

3 DAYS LEFT IN RED KING CRAB SEASON

National Weather Service Advisory: W WINDS RANGING
FROM 40-50 KT 5-0 KNOTS. SEAS 26 FT.

Tom decided to call his wife because he had an hour between
two strings of pots. The wind was blowing and the boat swayed,
causing Tom to feel like he was sitting on top of a rocking chair.
He tried to call her a few times a week while he was away, just to
check in and let her know everything was all right. He wanted to
call more but he would just miss her more. It was hard enough
being on the boat already.

Then again, he thought, there wasn't much time left on the
boat. He would try her when they were heading back to port to
drop off their catch.

THE DAY BEFORE RED KING CRAB SEASON ENDS

National Weather Service Advisory: NW WINDS RANGING
FROM 55-65 KT 6-5 KNOTS. SEAS 32 FT. FREEZING SPRAY

The wind was whipping starboard to port, rocking the boat side
to side while waves pounded it front to back. Ice built up on the
starboard side from the freezing rain.

Tom hated to send his men on deck in horrible weather and
under dangerous conditions, but if they didn't start hammering,
the ice would weigh the boat down until it capsized.

"Gentlemen," Tom said over the intercom. "Because of the
weather, this request is voluntary. I need some of you guys to go
out and pound the ice off the boat. It's shitty out there so put on
extra gear and your life vests. Nick and Max, knock the ice off in
the middle first. You guys know the drill."

Nick, Max and Alexander sat in the gear room getting ready.
Mike had found some work to do in the engine room. None of
the men complained because he had seniority. The greenhorn
chose to stay in his bunk, guaranteeing he wouldn't be back next

season. If he couldn't get past his fear for himself, he needed to get past it for the other men on the boat.

"You boys ready?" Nick said, rubbing his hands together with a smile.

Alexander and Max sighed in unison.

A gust of wind sucked Nick's breath away as soon as he stepped on deck. The rocking of the boat caused the men to stagger like children learning to walk. With each step they were forced to catch their balance before taking another. The pots were collecting ice in the webbing. Most of them had so much ice the netting looked like a wall with all the holes filled in.

The three men pounded at the ice with rubber mallets. Nick stood on a crab pot trying to get the ice off the top of the stack, while Max and Alexander pounded the ice in the middle of the boat. As soon as they started on a new section, the one they had just finished had began to accumulate more ice.

The men heard the grind of metal on metal, and then all was silent. They looked at Tom in the crow's nest.

"What the hell?" Max said.

Tom leaned his head out the window and shouted "Keep chopping!" before running to the engine room.

Out of habit he stopped to put on ear protection before realizing he didn't need it.

"What happened?" he asked, walking into the room.

"I think we blew a piston," Mike said, shaking his head. "I'm pretty sure that the bilge pump is broken as well. I don't know. I need a little more time."

"We don't have time."

"Call it in then."

"Fuck." Tom smacked his open palm on the wall. The only time he had ever called in for help was when he had Chuck go overboard. On his way back upstairs, Tom noticed Sarah sitting at the kitchen table, smoking a cigarette and having a cup of coffee.

"That quiet you hear is the sound of a dead boat in a fucking Arctic hurricane. Get your ass out there and start whacking at ice or the boat's going to capsize." Tom glared at Sarah. "Move!"

Sarah shot up and hustled to the gear room.

"Mayday, Mayday, Mayday. This is Captain Tom Staley on the Ms. Remorse, Ms. Remorse, Ms. Remorse. MMSI 367363350."

Tom let go of the talk button to make sure the line was still open. He was the only boat requesting backup.

"We're taking on water," Mike said from behind him. "We need to get everyone in their suits."

Tom stared at the men on deck. "Go," he said without turning around.

"Mayday. The Ms. Remorse is dead in the water. Position 51 53 North, 179 39 West, bearing three hundred and forty degrees, drifting at two knots. We are a fishing vessel. We've blown our engine and we're taking on water. We have six people on board. The boat is black with a white stripe on the hull. This is the Ms. Remorse, 367363350. Over."

"USCG to Ms. Remorse," a male voice said. "We'll send assistance immediately. Please remain on the radio for as long as it is safe to do so, over."

"Ms. Remorse to USCG," Tom said. "I'm glad you guys are out there. Over."

"USCG to Ms. Remorse. We are scrambling the chopper now. We are going to try to get there in under an hour. Is your boat going to stay above water that long?"

"Not a chance USCG."

"Copy that Ms. Remorse. Do you have flares?"

"Roger. We have four of them."

"Okay Ms. Remorse. Don't use them until you can hear the helicopter. If you do we won't be able to pick you guys up until it's light out, and we have a dozen hours before the sun comes up."

The boat had been headed bow-first into the waves before it lost power. Before long the wind and the water turned the boat sideways and the waves crashed against its side. The men were forced into the gear room for safety.

All the men were pulling on their red survival suits when Tom came in. He looked each member of his crew in the eyes.

"Don't worry men," Tom said. "These suits are just a safety precaution." Tom didn't even believe himself when he said it so he knew no one else did either.

The boat groaned and tilted to one side, causing the men to lean against the slant for a second before it righted. Some of the extra hats, gloves and boots fell out of the cubbyholes.

"Aren't you supposed to go down with the ship Captain?" Nick said with a gleam in his eyes.

"Fuck this hunk of scrap metal," Tom responded. "This boat has taken enough of my life. I have a wife to go home to."

Nick and Max went to the supply closet to find the survival raft.

"Who stacked these boxes on top of the raft that's supposed to save our lives?" Max said. "Help me move this shit."

"You did," Nick replied. "You dummy. I told you not to do that."

The boat rolled to a sixty-degree angle to the port side and stayed.

The men lumbered back into the gear room, using one hand to carry the raft and the other to brace themselves against the wall.

"This thing is pretty light," Max said.

"Everyone has to hold on to it," Tom said. "It's not even forty pounds. See this cord? We pull it and it inflates in ten seconds."

In the gear room Alexander had his head in his hands. Mike walked over to him.

"You just gotta breathe, buddy," he said, putting his hand on his shoulder.

"Whoever gets inside first, crawl to the back so that there's room for everyone else," Tom said. "We need the raft to be weighed down as quickly as possible. There's ten feet of rope inside, so tie it under your armpits so that we don't lose the raft in the wind."

The boat tilted to farther to an eighty-degree angle. The men heard dishes and other utensils falling on the floor in the kitchen.

Sarah took a knee in the middle of the circle of men and closed his eyes. "Lord, please keep us all safe..."

Nick walked out into the hallway. He refused to ask for help from a maker who put him in the situation to begin with. He waited to step back into the gear room until he heard the "Amen."

"Here we go," Tom said, looking at Max, then Nick.

The men huddled at the door leading to the deck. Nick pushed it open like they were a SWAT team invading a drug dealer's house. They were immediately greeted by a gale force wind that sent Alexander's orange winter hat sailing into the sea. Max was the last out of the gear room, while Tom backed out with the other side of the raft.

Nick and Max were on their knees when a wave hit the deck, knocking over Alexander, Mike and Sarah. Within seconds they all scrambled to their feet and surrounded the raft.

Nick stood up to get his bearings when another wave crashed on his back, driving his head and shoulders into the deck. He laid on his stomach, woozy, watching Max inflate the raft. The other men had managed to brace themselves for the wave.

Through blurry and wet eyes, Nick watched as Max came over, and picked him up.

"You okay?" Max said. "Dad doesn't look so hot."

Blood ran from Nick's forehead and into his eyes as he watched Max put his arm around his father.

Sarah tossed the inflated raft over the side of the boat and tied it to the rail. The boat was leaning and he was able to make the 20-foot jump off the railing and land on the roof of the watercraft. Then he scrambled through the portal and disappeared inside.

The boat shifted further to the port side.

Alexander stood motionless, stunned by the madness surrounding him.

The boat's lights flickered and for a moment they were plunged into total darkness.

"We need to get the fuck off of this boat," Mike yelled at Alexander, grabbing him by the arm and leading him to the rail. "You got me chief?"

Alexander nodded. He looked over the side of the boat at the raft and backed up a step.

"Either jump or I'm going to have to throw you," Mike said.

A few of the crab pots from the top of the stack fell onto the deck, causing a loud clang and snapping Alexander out of his daze. When he jumped, only half of his body made it onto the raft. He struggled to get on before Sarah's arm shot out of the portal, grabbed him by the back of his survival suit and pulled him in. Once Alexander was in, Mike followed him overboard and onto the raft.

Nick stumbled over to Tom and Max.

Max yelled something that disappeared into the howling wind.

"What?" Nick yelled back.

"We need to get Dad on the raft," Max said.

"How?"

"We'll get him as close as we can. If he doesn't make it we will go in after him."

Nick looked at the raft and Mike peeked his head out. He nodded as if he had heard their conversation.

More pots fell from the stack onto the deck and into the water. The boat leaned to a 45-degree angle.

All three men stood on the rail. Tom jumped and fell short of the boat. He plunged feet first into the water. Max leapt after him, shaking the rail and knocking Nick backward onto the deck.

One of the 700-pound pots slid into him, pinning his waist and his legs to the rail. Through his pain, he saw Max pull Tom into the raft, soaking wet.

Nick put both of his hands on the rail and began to push up, trying to wiggle his broken legs. After a few moments, he freed himself from under the pot.

He looked for a moment at the rope tying the raft to the boat. He knew he wouldn't be able to stand up on his broken legs and make the twenty foot jump. He knew that he if went over the side, he wouldn't be able to swim. He reached into his pocket and pulled out the folding knife that Tom had given him on his thirteenth birthday. As he cut the line to set the crew free, Nick thought of Madden saying that he knew Nick would take care of his father.

Nick cut the rope.

The survival raft floated away with the men watching out of the porthole. Max yelled something but it was lost in the wind.

Nick looked around. His only hope was a buoy. He crawled over to it using his arms and unlashed it from the deck.

The boat rolled further to its starboard side. Nick dragged his legs and the buoy up the slanted deck and grabbed onto the rail just as the boat turned completely on its side. He pulled himself over the rail.

Laying on the side of the boat he looked out into the water. He hoped the Coasties would hurry because he wouldn't last too long in the 30-degree water. He felt the boat slowly sink under him. He took the long rope that was tied around the top of the buoy and weaved it between his broken legs. Then he tied another knot on top of the buoy, lashing himself to it.

He gripped the buoy with both hands as the ship disappeared from under him. The mermaid that he had welded onto the front of the boat was the last part to go under. He thought, three months worth of work just went down the drain. A wave sent him rolling backwards. He went under, then over, the buoy.

Cold water ran into his nose and mouth. His suit filled with water at the cuffs at his hands and feet and he started to shiver. The knot tethering him to the buoy was coming undone.

As he tried to get his freezing hands to tighten the knot, another wave came and slammed the buoy into his face. Even though he was too numb from the cold to feel pain, his vision blurred and his vision became tunneled on his left side. He tried to hold onto the knot with both hands but he could feel it slipping.

The next wave separated him from the buoy. He started to swim after it but his boots and jacket were heavy with water.

He was surrounded by darkness.

He tried to get his broken legs to kick to stay on the surface, but he couldn't feel if they moved.

While he was sinking, he held his breath. He thought of fishing with Max and Tom. He thought about how the Staleys came to the hospital after the shooting and took him in.

Then he inhaled.

It was a gorgeous day out for December. The air was chilly and crisp without a cloud in the sky. The sun warmed the sunroom enough so that Carol only had to wear a hooded sweatshirt.

It was one of the shirts that Tom would give the crew at the end of the fishing season. The shirt said "F/V Ms. Remorse" with a drawing of the boat that one of the former crewmembers had done. She had joked to Tom that she wanted a pink version for the wives, but he laughed it off and told her that the sweatshirts were earned on the boat.

When she said that she thought she had earned one as his wife, he gave her his. She waited until he left for the season and then wore it when she missed him. It felt a little silly, like something a high school girl would do with a boy's letter jacket, but it also made her feel a little closer to him.

She was having a glass of lemonade when the phone rang. As she reached for the phone she saw the caller ID: "USCG-Kodiak."

She knew the United States Coast Guard's Kodiak station was the search and rescue for the boats in Alaska. It was well-known to the wives of fishermen and crabbers that the Coasties didn't make social calls. The call meant that either her husband's boat was in Davy Jones's Locker or on its way there.

Her eyes got wet and a solitary tear ran down her face. She forced herself to pick up the phone on the third ring.

"Hello?"

News Release

Coast Guard rescues five from sinking vessel 113 miles
southwest of St. Paul Island

Kodiak, Alaska – A Coast Guard Air Station Sitka MH-60
Jayhawk helicopter crew rescued five men from the 112-foot
fishing vessel Ms. Remorse after the crew reported their vessel
was taking on water 113 miles southwest of St. Paul Island. One
member of the crew perished. The crew member's name will be
released pending familial notification.

The USCG-Kodiak received notification of the incident via
an urgent marine information broadcast.

The Jayhawk located and hoisted the crew from the Ms.
Remorse after it sank. They were safely transferred to Adak
Island.

The Ms. Remorse's crew reported they were able to shut off
the fuel valves before the vessel sank. The helicopter crew
reported a light sheen near the vessel. The crew reported that
approximately 220 gallons of diesel fuel are on board the Ms.
Remorse. Coast Guard Marine Safety Detachment Ketchikan
personnel will investigate the cause of the sinking.

ABOUT THE AUTHOR

Clayton Hanson was born and raised in Alaska. He enjoys naps and pizza. For the past four years he has worked as a writer and editor for a news service providing analysis and information about Congress in Washington, D.C.
He can be found at Facebook.com/Hanson.Clayton and on Twitter @SnuffyMcDuffy.